A NEARBY COUNTRY CALLED LOVE

A NEARBY COUNTRY
CALLED LOVE

Salar Abdoh

VIKING

VIKING
An imprint of Penguin Random House LLC
penguinrandomhouse.com

All translations from Arabic of *The Stations* of al-Niffari (tenth century) by Salar Abdoh.

LIBRARY OF CONGRESS CATALOGING-IN-PUBLICATION DATA
Names: Abdoh, Salar, author.
Title: A nearby country called love: a novel / Salar Abdoh.
Description: [New York] : Viking, [2023]
Identifiers: LCCN 2023015908 (print) | LCCN 2023015909 (ebook) |
ISBN 9780593653906 (hardcover) | ISBN 9780593653913 (ebook)
Subjects: LCSH: Families—Iran—Fiction. | Iranians—Fiction. |
Iran—Social conditions—Fiction. | LCGFT: Novels.
Classification: LCC PS3551.B2687 N43 2023 (print) |
LCC PS3551.B2687 (ebook) | DDC 813/.54—dc23/eng/20230407
LC record available at https://lccn.loc.gov/2023015908
LC ebook record available at https://lccn.loc.gov/2023015909

Printed in the United States of America
1st Printing

DESIGNED BY MEIGHAN CAVANAUGH

Babak and Bahar,

thank you for the door you opened

so that this book could be written.

Once you see me not behind a veil and not behind a name, you will have seen me absolutely.

The Stations of al-Niffari (tenth century)

PART ONE

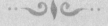

One

Issa saw that that word—*burn*—had lately turned into a refrain for his friend, always hovering on the tip of his tongue, starting with a fire Nasser had fought down in the Zamzam district in south Tehran. Nasser knew the family of the burned woman, knew the piece of shit who drove her to pour gasoline on herself on the thirteenth day of the Persian New Year, the start of spring, when folks head to the parks to celebrate and throw bad luck into the wind.

He'd gone over to Beirut to search for love and had come back empty-handed, as usual. Nasser was there to pick him up from the airport. He broke the news that they'd have all day to rest before they had to head down to the Zamzam district to fight for the "honor" of a woman Issa had never known existed until now. It was bullshit, this chivalry. They were going to act out a scene of street theater only to flaunt themselves and not save any woman's honor. This was the second time in four months that Nasser had asked him for backup in some skirmish like that.

Nasser didn't really need the backup, yet he insisted on it. Maybe because the world of men could be pretty barren until men found each other. Which was rare. Mostly it was a relentless loneliness that one made up for with bravado in places like Jomhuri Avenue, where Issa had found himself selling expensive, Korean-made washing machines and refrigerators alongside Nasser for the last year. He had been kicked out of his university job because someone in the Selection Department had complained about his godlessness. That was what they called it—*godlessness*. He wasn't sure where exactly the complaint had come from, and at that point, he didn't care. There was always a complaint, always someone out to get you because they could. It didn't matter where you lived or what wind of grievance blew your way. Still, Issa knew a couple of foreign languages, so a Good Samaritan at the university who felt sorry about the injustice from the Selection Committee had said they were looking for someone who could speak with embassy folk shopping along Jomhuri Avenue. The Russians, Italians, Turks, British, French, and Germans all had their embassies down around Jomhuri, and their people needed fridges and washing machines, didn't they? Turned out none of them came to buy a damn thing at all, but there he had met Nasser, who was moonlighting during his forty-eight-hour off-shifts from his job as a fireman.

Then he'd backed Nasser in a fight.

Or rather, he'd executed an instance of precise violence in the other man's place. Precise because Issa knew how to do it. He'd been trained in the art long ago and could still be quite good at it. And because violence was the glue that held their inadequate lives together. It wasn't a way of life; it was life itself. And if Issa had at one time tried to escape that life, it was only because he'd been led to believe there were other options for men like them.

There weren't.

That first time, a customer was slapping his own little boy on the back of the neck repeatedly while negotiating the price of a vacuum cleaner. Nasser had followed the man outside, and Issa followed Nasser onto Jomhuri Avenue, amid the thick crowds hustling cell phones and electronic paraphernalia underneath the Hafez Overpass.

Nasser catches up to the man, who looks like he is about to smack the boy again.

"What's going on? Has the kid broken your phone? Did he shit on your couch?"

The man—big, flabby, his face oxlike—is disoriented for a second and asks if he left something in the store.

"You did, you whore's son. You left a bad taste, is what you left in the store. What has the boy done that you keep hurting him like that?"

Issa stands there watching, near two policemen who know Nasser well enough to realize this is not yet their business, and, for the time being, they shouldn't butt in. The southwest corner of Jomhuri and Hafez is surely one of the most crowded thoroughfares in all of the Middle East. But where they stand, next to one of the fat pillars of the overpass, there's space enough for anything. Issa watches the little boy—eight or nine at most. Already at that age he looks like life has beaten him down. If he knows how to smile, Issa doesn't see it. This boy is soft. He lacks the rough unruliness boys his age possess. He is not ever going to get in fistfights and make his old man proud. Which is why the father treats the kid as he does. The man wants to unsoften the boy. And suddenly Issa wants Nasser to really hurt this man. Just plain flatten him. In fact, all the bitterness of the past several years funnels into this moment, and he recalls, for the umpteenth time, his flight from New York City back to Iran, a country he had not seen for over a decade—his crime a few street-bought antianxiety pills that turned up during a random search at a train station, which in turn became a ridiculous charge of drug possession by a noncitizen.

Then a one-way ticket east. To here. To this corner of Jomhuri and Hafez.

"Son." Nasser addresses the little boy gently. "Is this man your father?"

The boy nods.

"Let go of his hand and go stand to the side for a minute, by those nice policemen."

The man finally gets it. Amazingly, he actually lets go of the boy's hand. But then he says, "I'm going to go right back into your store and get you fired."

"You can try. Nothing will come of it. I'm their best salesman. They don't fire good salesmen. And where do you think you are, Germany? This is Tehran, you idiot."

The man now looks in Issa's direction as if wanting confirmation of all this, and Issa gives it. "He's not going to get fired for ruining your face. He might go to jail for two days or two weeks, but he'll have his job when he comes back out. And he'll find you again."

"What do you guys want from me?"

"Not to hit the boy."

Before the man has a chance to say that it is not anyone's business, Nasser adds, "Everything is my business. Your kid especially."

Issa watches, listens. The father is the embodiment of all the things that are wrong with all of them. The man's greasy hair no doubt smelling of onions and the sulfurous reek of yesterday's kebab. The entire thing happens in less than five minutes. The policemen who have had enough amusement and must return to their clogged traffic finally intervene. They're not going to let Nasser beat this guy. Nasser's hands are far too heavy and relentless; everyone on Jomhuri Avenue knows this. It will be ugly. They agree that, instead, Issa must accompany the two-bit tyrant to one of the back alleys off Hafez, below the new monster mall that only sells cell phones. What is planned there is anybody's guess. A chat perhaps. Or an exchange of money that Issa will then give to the cops for their time and trouble and, supposedly, looking out for the boy. But Ali the lockpick is there, like always. So is the one-eyed war vet who runs a discount grill from the back of his blue truck for the neighborhood drug addicts. And, of course, the addicts themselves, crazy-eyed, subdued, and hollow-cheeked.

This is where I shipped myself back to?

And then he applies what he knows best, a bone-crushing front kick to the man's knee. It is the definition of precision, this kick, which he first learned from his old man thirty years earlier when he was a nine-year-old boy watching his father run a Shotokan karate academy below their two-bedroom apartment in the working-class district of Monirieh. But there's nothing heroic in what Issa has done, and he knows it. The blow is mostly an expression of frustration. Still, it feels good when the man buckles and Issa tells one of the junkies to come up and give the fool a slap on the back of the head. "How does it feel to be on the receiving end for a change, *gaav*, you dumb cow?"

Later he tells Nasser, "We didn't do that boy any favors. You realize this, don't you?"

"Why do you say that?"

"That no-good bastard will take it out on the kid."

Nasser considers this. "How bad did you hurt him?"

"I think I broke his leg. Maybe."

"You know how to fight?"

"My father ran a karate school in Monirieh. I grew up around that stuff."

"It actually works? Karate, I mean."

"It did today."

Nasser sighs. "I wish we'd taken his address. You really think he'll hurt the boy?"

"He'll think twice about humiliating the kid in public from now on. That's something."

"Really? That's enough?"

"It's never enough."

His violence had been juvenile, he knew. But you simply had to believe sometimes—believe you could be doing a lot worse than the bad you'd already harvested. That was what he'd done when they'd told him he could hire a lawyer and beat the flimsy charge against him so he could remain in America. It had taken all of two seconds to decide he didn't want a lawyer and he didn't want to stay. Why all the fuss? He had been working the night shift in a hotel for the last eight years. Everyone he worked with was an immigrant like him. Chinese, African, Eastern European, Latin—

all of them hustling for the next two-dollar tip on a four-hundred-dollar-a-night room. Maybe there was a transcendent story of emigration and success somewhere on the horizon, but Issa hadn't found it yet and wanted no part of it now. His rent was too high—that was what mattered. His overpriced rat-trap hole-in-the-wall walk-up in the Bronx.

No. Sometimes there simply was no story of triumphing elsewhere in the world. Home was where one belonged, even if home was shit. And a decade had been more than enough for the flower of disillusion to turn into a forest.

Besides, work the graveyard shift for six months and even the air you take in begins to feel different; work it for eight years and you turn into a sleepwalker prone to seeking a cornucopia of deadening medicines. It was those meds that had gotten him thrown out of America, and he was not ungrateful for it. He'd gone back to the furnished, fully paid-for apartment that he'd shared with his dead father and dead brother in Monirieh and begun from zero, again. Besides selling washing machines, he slowly made up for the loss of the university job by teaching English courses and the conversational Spanish he'd picked up through years of working in hotels alongside Central Americans. Nowadays he taught in one of the better private language institutes in the city. The pay wasn't bad and his apartment was, after all, his own. He wasn't lacking. He didn't have love—true—but he was working on it.

HE ROLLED THE WINDOW DOWN. It was four in the morning and the desert air between the airport and the city smelled like desperation. He thought of all the men and women, himself included, who had tried their luck at being elsewhere in the world, all of them taking this same road to the airport and eventually being turned back from one country or another, penniless and broken—statuses denied, work permits not renewed, lives gone from nothing to nowhere.

The monumental Imam Khomeini shrine, just past the toll-booths at the threshold of the city, had a crushing presence at that hour. He was scared of the place and drawn to it at the same time. It had nothing to do with the larger-than-life fellow who was buried there and after whom the adjacent airport was named; rather, it was the sense that you could build sacredness out of nothing—one day there would be mud and dust in a place in the middle of nowhere, and a few years later pilgrims from the four corners of the earth would be flocking to those fresh minarets and domes, weeping as if this were a place as old as the stories of Hagar and Abraham.

He could not quite fathom any of this except to maybe pay some homage. Not quite a believer, and not quite enjoying the luxuries of disbelief either.

Nasser said, "I still don't understand what's in Beirut for you."

"The possibility of love."

"You are a donkey."

He wasn't going to argue the point. Nasser would not understand if he tried to explain that the love he sought was tied up in something as baroque as literary translation. The firehouse captain would simply call Issa a donkey again. How to explain to a guy like Nasser that you could actually give up years of martial arts practice for literature's sake. It was futile. Issa's grandfather had been a Shia cleric who had walked all the way from down south in the Lorestan province to Tehran. He had written books of Islamic Sharia law in Arabic that Issa still kept in Monirieh but had not been able to read until just a few years ago. His generation no longer had command of the Holy Book—it was like having a limb cut off, part of one's self gone. So during all those years of the graveyard shift at the hotel when there were crawling hours of free time, he'd sat down to steep himself in the language of the Koran, in America of all places. Not because he had faith, but in fact because he did not have it. The immigrant life mostly took from you, just milked you dry. But if you learned the ways of another place, you might take a little back. America had not been ungenerous that way, even if it had eventually kicked him out. He had even started to take graduate courses toward another useless college degree while sleepwalking the daylight hours far from the hotel.

In Arabic he recited, *"The beloveds are those whom we do not gaze upon."*

Nasser cursed under his breath. "You go to Beirut for four days and you can't speak Persian anymore? What is it you mumbled?"

Issa told him.

"You really are a donkey."

"Brother Nasser, those words were translated by a woman whom I wish to love."

"When did you meet her?"

"I haven't. Not yet."

Nasser shook his head, exasperated. "Look, we have a fight tonight. Correction: I have a fight. You are there for backup, in case those fatherless whores decide to jump me. Here." He reached across the dashboard, brought out a small pouch, and told Issa to open it. "Take that box cutter in there. If they decide to go with weapons, they'll use daggers. They always do in Zamzam, those rotten lowlifes. But we're not going to use daggers. All right? Just box cutters."

"Nasser, you want me to watch your back in a place like Zamzam against people with daggers with only a box cutter? Have you lost your mind?"

"No, it's you who has lost his mind. This so-called beloved of yours is in Beirut?"

"I think so."

"So you don't even know where she is? She probably lied."

Yes, it appeared that she had. And who she was, Issa still had no idea. He'd been catching her periodic translations from Arabic into Persian in one of the literary journals. But when he contacted the magazine, no one seemed to know who this translator was. There was only an email address. He had written and she replied immediately. Her name was Maysa. From Beirut. So, just as Nasser said, like a fool he'd gone there to try to find her. But the address she'd given in the Dahieh district in south Beirut didn't exist. After a half hour of wandering aimlessly on foot, he was picked up by a Hezbollah security detail. This was their territory and the militia had eagle eyes on every block. What was he doing walking aimlessly in Dahieh? He'd told them the truth: love had brought him here. He was looking for Maysa; he showed them her poetry translations from a copy of the journal he'd brought along. They laughed, slapped him on the back, took him out for lunch, and finally said, "Brother, you are a child. There's no such address. No such Maysa here in Dahieh, or we'd know. We know every single poet in Dahieh. And every single snitch. And every single translator. And every Romeo. And now we know you. Go home and look for love where you can find it."

Nasser was gunning the engine, the road mostly empty at that early hour except for the string of airport taxis on the Persian Gulf Highway. Before long they were in Monirieh, where nearly all the shuttered shops on the main avenue were sporting goods stores. A few years before Issa was born, his father had set up the dojo below their apartment, at a time when kung fu and karate were just starting to make their way into the country. During those early years there were only a handful of other Japanese hard-style dojos in Tehran. This gave the old man cachet, even though after the revolution they'd tried more than once to take over the dojo and throw him in jail because of his past. The only son of a cleric, he should have followed in his own father's footsteps. Instead he'd become a professional military man, where he first learned karate from some of the Americans who had been stationed there in those days, and later he'd gone to Japan to study the art in depth. All this should have gotten him killed after the revolution, since his loyalties obviously lay elsewhere. But he was a child of the neighborhood and beloved by his Shotokan disciples. By the time he'd started letting Issa into the dojo for practice, the dust of the politics around them had finally settled. Meantime, Issa's mother passed before the boy saw his second birthday, and his older brother had no interest at all in the compulsory swagger of their traditional south-central Tehran neighborhood.

A triangle of a father and two sons at odds with themselves and their closed-in, womanless universe.

The dojo was still there, empty. But it was still Issa's property. As soon as he'd come back from New York a local boss had tried to strong-arm him into selling that prime space with its two access points to the main avenue. When he tried to get the *shahrkhar* off his back by promising to think about it, the guy had his men spread the old story of Issa's brother being a *kooni*, a fag, as they called him, as the main reason their father had died so early, from heartbreak.

You would think these things were nothing, and that the world was a whole lot different now. But these things were everything in a neighborhood like Monirieh. And the world, Issa knew, was still mostly like Monirieh, not the New York he'd been living in. Those first times he saw men walking arm in arm, kissing each other, calling each other husband or wife at the hotel, he'd felt envy and then a recollection of grief for his dead brother. He wished for his brother, Hashem, to have had a semblance of what these couples had, if only for a day—even if he didn't quite understand it all himself, even if it was as far from the world he had halfheartedly chained himself to during those last years that their father ran the dojo and pretended not to know his older son at all.

He would not forgive the Monirieh neighborhood for any of this, though he still knew each nook and cranny of each sporting goods store by heart. He could fight off an army of *madar*-fuckers who came at his door accusing the old man of having been an American stooge back in the day, but to bring up the past about his dead brother made everybody go back to bad old ghosts. He didn't want this. What he wanted was peace and to be left alone mostly. Yes, his brother was gay—a queer, fag, fairy, or whatever else they would call him; and he'd loved him not because he was or wasn't, but because they were brothers. Period. And since the day he'd opened his eyes in Monirieh until the day they finally killed Hashem, he'd had fights on his brother's behalf because, well, that's what brothers did for brothers.

Parked in front of his building, the only other people they saw were the municipality's night workers sweeping the streets and collecting the garbage. They looked like little worker bees wearing face masks and yellow vests. He loved this city, to a point. He was and wasn't glad to be back. It was the kind of place that made you imagine apocalypse had actually arrived, and it wasn't impossible to live through it after all.

Nasser pointed to the empty dojo space. "I don't know why you don't sell the place. You won't have to work another day if you do that. What's keeping you, Issa?"

"Sentimental value."

"You are such a damn donkey. You are sitting on real estate people would sell their mother for. They'd sell their grandmother too."

He had already told Nasser about the local *shahr-khar*. They called him Haj Davood. Usually between six and nine p.m. you could find the guy in a real estate joint he owned just below Monirieh Square. He sat behind his fat desk gaping at his fingers and the fat, expensive rings on them, talking property and laughing over tired jokes with cronies and ass-kissers. The bodybuilding gym across the street also belonged to him. Property like Issa's didn't get sold without his approval. Haj Davood could make a buyer change their mind quickly.

"Nasser, you already know my situation."

"So sell it to the *shahr-khar*."

"He wants it for a song. My father ran himself to the ground over that place. It's all I have in the world."

"Rent it then."

"Haj Davood would make sure the tenant doesn't pay me after the second month and then doesn't leave."

"Then I'm going to have a talk with the man."

"You can't solve all the problems of this city with your fists, you know. The guy owns people." After a pause Issa added, "Why are we in a fight tonight? I mean, I know why. But is it necessary? The woman—Khoda, have mercy on her soul—is burned and gone already."

"Shut your damn mouth. Don't speak about the dead that way."

"Sorry."

"Khoda, have mercy . . ."

Nasser's voice trailed off. He had a reputation to uphold. He'd worked his way up the chain of command to become a captain in Tehran's sprawling customs firehouse, where the opportunity for theft was too good to avoid. All that merchandise coming in and leaving the capital had to pass under the nose of the firehouse command. They couldn't have an honest captain on the job, so the higher-ups had nudged him to move, and he'd leveraged that into a transfer to his own neighborhood. But these kinds of moves, like Issa's return to Tehran, always had a cost. In Monirieh, Issa still had to protect the past without batting an eye, having an "anti-revolutionary" father, a *kooni* brother; he had to be prepared to brawl at the mention of either of their names in any way less than respectful. If he didn't, he'd be eaten alive. It was an exhausting man-eat-man world that made you want to run away. He had already done that once; he wouldn't be doing it again.

He watched Nasser. The absurdity of their hollow lives as men of the Middle East. In the Zamzam district, a guy like Nasser cultivated the notion that protecting the weak was not a fairy tale, but rather an occupation, a religion. An exhausting idea of valor that Persian classical literature had ingrained in their brains since first grade, and they'd foolishly bought into and still believed in. Maybe they were obsolete men that way, living in a world that had already left them behind. Yet what other choice did they have?

He asked Nasser, "Let's say you beat up this guy today within an inch of his life, is it going to bring back his burned wife?"

"You don't have to stand next to me tonight if you don't want to."

A police car slowed down parallel to them. Nasser flashed his fireman's badge and nodded. They nodded back and drove on. Issa's mind wandered. He recalled his meager life as a hotel clerk in America. The place had been in the heart of Manhattan, and its old bar was famous as a drinking hole for legendary American writers going back several generations. This was a piece of information he carried inside him like a life jacket, as if he had been part of something bigger than being a mere night clerk with the lazy Middle Eastern accent whom drunken guests flirted with at three a.m.

He said to Nasser, "Do you know how many women burn themselves in this country every day?"

"And every time a woman burns herself, the world ends."

It was a thought. Issa had to consider it. He said nothing.

"Maybe you are just scared," Nasser went on.

"You know I'm not."

"Your karate is shit, brother."

"That I already know. But I'm talking about tonight—why this fight in particular?"

"She was a distant relative."

"You lie. You didn't mention that before."

"I don't lie. Zamzam is full of people from my hometown. She is a distant relative. But that's not actually why we're fighting tonight."

Issa waited for him to continue.

"Remember when the Plasco building burned down?"

Issa remembered. It had been a few months back. Seventeen stories high, on the other side of Jomhuri Avenue across from the Friday Bazaar, Plasco was the first building of its kind in Tehran. This had been long before the revolution. But by the time it burned, the old structure was an oddity superseded by far more modern buildings. It had housed little shops and garment manufacturing outfits paying negligible rent and not budging from there. They said the place was burned on purpose. Whatever it was, it was a nightmare to witness during and afterward, like the World Trade Center in miniature, fire smoldering and breaking out again and again over the course of several weeks and making everyone in the vicinity sick.

Nasser looked hard at him. "I can still smell that burned flesh at Plasco. It's still with me. You understand? And when I smell that smell, which is all the time, I remember that poor woman."

There was nothing to say to that. Issa slid out of the car and grabbed his carry-on suitcase from the back seat.

"I'll pick you up at seven," Nasser called out. "Get some sleep. Don't forget the box cutter."

When the other man was gone, rather than going upstairs to the apartment, Issa unlocked the dojo and went inside. Fighting had a particular taste and smell. Practicing for fighting added a layer of scent that suggested fatigue and fear. After all these years the dojo still carried that tang. A karate academy in this neighborhood had meant brawls. And to be able to protect Hashem he had to be as unlike his brother as he could. It was the only logic of the geography he knew and had been taught. One time, a boy in tenth grade had tried to kiss him as a joke. Issa had smashed the kid's nose. Sent him flying into a desk with a side-kick in front of their classmates and was about to hit him again when a passing teacher had stopped him. When they'd called his father to the school, there was that smirk and look of pride on the old man's face.

How he had hated that smirk, and for the next two weeks he could hardly look his own brother in the face. When he finally did, Hashem said, "I heard you almost killed a kid for trying to kiss you. They are talking about it on the street."

"The guy's a bully. I taught him a lesson."

"No, Issa. That isn't it."

"What is it then?"

"You don't want to be a fag like me."

"Don't say these things, Hashem."

"That word bothers you?" His brother got close and planted a kiss right on his face. "How about this? Does that bother you? You want to make the old man proud you're not *kooni* like your older brother? Is he proud of you now?"

"He is."

Hashem had slapped him then, and he'd taken it.

So many years later, so little had actually changed. They were still brawling, the little men that they were. Here in Monirieh, over there in Zamzam. Backing Nasser in a dubious fight over a dead woman, or that day he had broken the man's knee under the

Hafez Overpass. It was all so formulaic. The things you owed to those you'd loved. And how he wanted to love. To really love. To taste it instead of the savageries of the everyday here. He didn't want to join Nasser in that stupid brawl in Zamzam; he didn't owe the burned woman anything. Except that he did. He owed her everything. They all did. He turned out the lights at the dojo, took in its stale sourness one more time, and then went upstairs to try to get some sleep before the fight.

Two

They stood by a small underpass off the highway. Nearby was a park, but it was drizzling and nobody wanted to fight in the open. There were a good fifty people there, not a woman among them. Kids chewing gum and horsing around. Several men had taken out a foldout table and passed around a *kalian* as if this were just a night out on the town.

Such things didn't happen quite like this in Tehran. It was like some *West Side Story* with shifted topography, an element of unreality filling the air, especially with those little kids milling about. An installation was what it was, self-conscious, wrong. The hookah, the gathering under a mostly disused tunnel. The futile maleness of it all, even if the whole act was supposedly over the honor of a woman.

There was no need for the box cutter Nasser had given him. This was a carnival. Issa wondered where they had buried the burned wife of the *madar*-fucker he was looking at. The widower seemed sedate, almost condescending, standing among a circle of men who looked Nasser's way but didn't say much. Nasser, meanwhile, was

SALAR ABDOH

pacing back and forth like something rabid. Issa watched resignedly, feeling sorry for his friend and himself. If they were righting something in this world, he felt foolish about it. Probably Nasser did, too, at this point. He had slept poorly all afternoon and wanted now to crawl back to bed and stop dwelling on Beirut and his unrequited love of a person he had never met.

Nasser finally started to walk toward the other man but had to stop and face a wall of young men who, despite everything, still remained deferential to the fire captain of Zamzam.

"Agha Nasser, we have respect for you in this neighborhood. Everyone does. My late wife, may she rest in peace, she was depressed. I didn't do that to her. She did it to herself."

The man pushed past the human wall and Issa got a better glimpse of him. Thicker in the shoulders than Nasser, he could have been just another bodybuilder in Monirieh. There were little bumps on the man's head where he obviously had had a recent cheap hair transplant. Beyond them, on both sides of the underpass, headlights shined past each other, and every time a car made to enter, it was directed to go the long way into Zamzam and avoid the tunnel.

Nasser said, "Why are you here, then? I sent word I wasn't coming here tonight just to talk."

"Talk is good. And I did nothing wrong. If you want us to hurt each other, it's all right with me. But what next? You want somebody to sing the legend of Agha Nasser in Zamzam? No problem, I'll sing it myself."

Several men laughed.

Nasser said something to the effect that he was going to snap the man's neck.

"Agha Nasser, my neck does not snap so easily. You can see, I'm not a little pushover. You think it's easy for me to come here and have to explain to you I didn't kill my wife? And why should I explain anything? You are not her brother."

"She was family."

"Being from the same town doesn't make her family. But I get it. You want to show the neighborhood these things can't happen on your watch. But you're only a firehouse captain here, not a king. You're just another guy like me." He gestured widely. "Like all of us here. I don't want to fight you. But . . ."

His voice drifted. The drizzle had turned into a downpour outside the tunnel, yet everyone waited intently. The bubble of the hookah had quieted and the little boys were looking wide-eyed at the two men, hungry for action.

For a moment, Issa imagined this big man was going to burst into tears. He looked genuinely stricken all of a sudden. Coming here, Issa had wanted to despise the guy, agitating himself into some kind of action. Now they all seemed like caricatures of men pretending at a fight. A woman had burned herself and they were going through the ritual of supposedly doing something about it. Yet it had nothing to do with her and everything to do with them, here, proving their prickly little manhoods. At that moment, it felt like Nasser and he were even bigger frauds than the fraudulent widower.

There was a loud bleep of a police siren, just once, before it went quiet. Its lights still flashing but staying outside the underpass. A few years back, when Issa was still in the States, this neighborhood was a haven for drug dealers. There had been turf wars and low-level crime syndicates. The municipality had cleaned things up and hanged rows of dealers right on the streets of Zamzam for the public to see. It was a way of showing muscle and making sure things stayed reasonable. This spectacle included men like Nasser doing their part to keep other men honest.

Tonight, Nasser had exceeded his authority.

What did it take for someone to get to the point of self-immolation? Try as he might, Issa couldn't fathom it. He recalled the Plasco building again. He hadn't smelled the burned flesh that Nasser had breathed in, but he thought he could taste it now, as an afterthought.

The man said, "It is not a crime to want to take a second wife."

There was a change, a strut to his words now, as if he were finally in his desired element. He even seemed affronted, wronged, playing the part of the pained survivor. It was the appearance of the police that had made him bold. He may have had his pals there with him, but all the rest of the people were here to watch Nasser get angry, fight, and win.

The police car just sat there, waiting. A repeat of that day a year earlier under the Hafez Overpass. Issa went up to Nasser and reached for his friend's wrist. Nasser didn't pull away.

"Let's go. We're done here. The man doesn't want to fight you."

Nasser eyed him as if in a trance. "It's my job. What do I tell her family?"

"Her family can worry about that. Not you. Come!"

Men began clapping. Sure, they'd come to see a fight, but now that it looked like it wasn't happening they wanted to imagine peace was just as sweet.

It wasn't. Not for them.

The widower said, "She set my house on fire, you know. She burned herself and burned my house. You think that's fair?"

"It's the least you deserve. What did you do to her beside pushing for a second wife?"

Those words had come from Issa's mouth, not Nasser's, and it took everyone, including Issa himself, by surprise.

The man grinned. "What? You saw the belt marks I left on her face too?"

The evil that the widower had just blurted—whether it was true or not—hovered like poison between them. Issa could tell even the men around him were shocked at those words—and with Nasser right there to hear it.

Yet all he could think to counter was to match the widower's horror with horror. "Yes, I saw the belt marks every time she called me over to your house when you weren't home, you son of a bitch."

They stared each other down, Issa surprised that the man wasn't coming at him with a cleaver. He surely would have if Nasser wasn't there.

This time it was Nasser who tugged at Issa, who was grateful. "Let's go. We're done here. I'll get this murdering bastard when I get him."

FOR THE SECOND TIME that Thursday, Nasser was dropping him off at home.

"I just can't get the smell of burned bodies off of me, Issa. It's killing me."

"Maybe you need to see someone."

"What? Like one of these people who take your money to talk to you?"

"Well, it's you who does the talking. They mostly just listen."

"I'm trying to be a decent man in this *kiri* town—a lame prick of a city if there ever was one. It's not easy to stay righteous here, you know. Why did you ever come back, Issa? You must have had a good life across the sea. Everybody wants to leave. Why return?"

"They didn't give me much choice. And they weren't exactly handing out gold coins over there."

Issa could tell the other man wanted to be invited upstairs for a couple of shots of raisin vodka. But he wasn't feeling it.

"Nasser, enough fights already," he pleaded. "All right?"

Nasser stared ahead of him past the steering wheel. The rain had stopped and the streets looked crisp, the thirsty asphalt quenched. "Why?" he asked.

"Because it's dumb. We're grown men."

"Grown men fight. Why do you think wars start?"

"You fought, or wanted to fight tonight, to save face. You didn't do it for that woman. If you hadn't gone and leaned on that guy's manhood, the whole neighborhood would have said Agha Nasser doesn't look after his own. You did this for you, not for her."

Nasser stared at him. "A man can fight for any number of reasons. Maybe I wanted to save face too. So what?"

There was no answer to that. Nasser's honesty didn't leave room for discussion. Now he was sighing.

"Look, I'll be thirty-six in a couple of months. My mother says she'll kill herself if I don't get married soon. And my father is *kiri* and a true asshole. But you? Why don't you get married?"

"I'm working on it."

Nasser laughed. "That no-show love affair you have going in Beirut?"

"We all have our thing."

"Our thing," Nasser repeated absently as he turned over the car engine.

HE COULDN'T BEAR going back to the apartment just yet. The apartment of the dead. When they'd been much younger he had shared the big bedroom with his older brother while their father took the small one in the back for himself. Issa recalled the bouts of barely controlled rage and weeping that ensued each time their old man thought his firstborn was not manly enough. It was a dance of endless humiliation between the two of them, starting in sixth grade for Hashem, when he came home from school one day and asked if he could take violin lessons. The old man, busy making a banana shake for Issa after having just taught an advanced karate class, raised his head and looked at Hashem, dumbstruck. Issa was almost two years younger and even then he understood something was not quite right with this picture. Within minutes they were downstairs at the dojo, where a few of the higher belts were still practicing. Hashem was made to punch the heavy bag until he was out of breath. Then the old man made him do the chicken walk a half dozen times around the dojo before putting him to spar with a teenage purple belt.

Hashem, who had always found excuses to avoid the dojo, stands there with a nervous smile on his face. Their father telling the other boy to attack. *Attack what?* Issa thinks to himself even then. *Attack Hashem's desire to learn the fucking violin?* He is nine years old and has been going to the dojo religiously for about half a year and wants to protect his brother but has no idea where his loyalty lies. He worships the old man and imagines what their father is doing will somehow cure Hashem of something. He does not know what that something is yet, but when he sees the other boy throwing a halfhearted *mawashigeri* roundhouse kick to the side of Hashem's face and pulling back at the last moment he wants to go out there and rip the boy's face apart, even though the other boy is twice his size. Suddenly, the old man's anger washes over them like wildfire. There are several other students in the dojo, standing mesmerized at this display of wrath by a sensei who has never before shown a lack of control in their presence. No one understands it. No one says a word. And then their father is raising his voice and warning the purple belt to either fight with his eldest son or never come back to the dojo again.

This time the boy attacks with a low *maegeri* front kick that catches Hashem in the inside thigh. The boy closes the distance and throws a lunge punch just above Hashem's right eye. He does not follow through with more punches, though. He looks embarrassed. And then Issa is running at him. The moves he has learned in the last half year at the dojo are out the window, and all he knows to do is to try to wrestle the kid by going for his legs.

The teenage boy shoos him off.

"Touch my brother again I'll kill you," he hears himself shouting ineffectively.

Hashem is rolled into a ball on the floor, holding his face, crying softly. Their father stands there with glass eyes, surely astounded at the wickedness he has just caused and looking as if he has just woken up from a bad dream. The purple belt bows and retreats.

The image stopped cold for Issa right there. He could not recall what had happened next. There was no talk of violin lessons ever again. Nor did their father ever lose his cool at the dojo like that again. But this was the last time Hashem stepped into that space. Something had been broken. And something had been built—a tall wall between them, for the remainder of the abbreviated lives of these two men, both of whom Issa had adored and who hated each other.

Then came the change in their bedroom arrangements. Issa had to move into the small bedroom by himself, and their father took the big bedroom and made Hashem his roommate. It was, in a way, the absolute worst punishment he could have inflicted on the two boys, taking away Hashem's privacy and at the same time forcing Issa, the younger brother, to have his. And the next few years turned into a cold war punctuated with bouts of seasonal brutality that ended in Hashem crying in one corner of the apartment and their father feeling remorse in another. At school, Hashem was beloved and, unlike Issa, a perfect student. The more their father heard praise from school about Hashem and his grades, the angrier he seemed to get, and he devised yet more tests of manhood, which Hashem failed at spectacularly. One day, the old man decided Hashem had to learn how to ride a motorcycle; it ended in the bike falling over Hashem and the hot exhaust scalding half his leg. More than once, the three of them had to go hiking in the mountains north of the city and learn to stake tents and shoot bows and arrows. Another failure. If Hashem didn't like karate, how about learning to box or wrestle or do judo? It was one thing after another, a desperate quicksand of man-making that always ended in disappointment and heartache. As time went by, Issa moved up through the ranks at the dojo and his belt colors changed. During the silent *mokuso* meditation intervals at the beginning and end of practice, he'd often wonder what their father was thinking. Did he think about Hashem then? Was his mind completely blank? Did he ever think about the men who still thought him an enemy of the revolution?

He had loved this man. And sometimes he hadn't. More than anything, he had wanted his father to love Hashem. Or at the very least cease trying to turn the older son into a version of himself. The wash of bad memories didn't fade with age but rather lingered and just grew more stale. Like the time after the old man put Hashem in a vicious chokehold up there in the mountains. Back at the apartment Issa had taken the small picture of the old man from his military days and ripped it in half. For days he'd hidden the photograph, ridden with guilt and fear that their father would find it. He did find it, years later. It was taped together but still showed the rip down the middle. The old man put the photo away and didn't ask about it, no doubt thinking it was Hashem who had wanted to destroy his mug and not the younger son.

What a relief when Hashem finally left home. As if a huge boulder that the three of them had been carrying was at last lifted. From his second year of high school, Hashem had refused to cohabit in the same room with the old man. To make peace, Issa had given him the small bedroom back and took to the sofa in the living room. Many nights he'd just go to the dojo and sleep there, leaving the old man and his brother to their silent revulsions. The stale scent of sweaty *gi* uniforms would always linger on his skin from those nights at the dojo. He had imagined even back then that the sourness was that of men's odium of one another. All men. It permeated everything, unwashable.

HE WALKED AIMLESSLY for a long time. The fasting month, Ramadan, would be coming around, and soon it would be summer. The previous summer had been unbearably hot, and tiny, white airborne creatures had invaded the city in swarms. They got into your mouth and hair and eyes, they stuck to car windshields and hung from trees. No one was sure what they were or where they had come from. It was a version of the day of the locusts but lasting an entire season in scorching heat. Sometimes he wondered if Hashem and their old man weren't better off gone from this world, or at least this city. Some of the old man's best martial arts students had eventually ended up running their own dojos. A few were famous now. Others notorious. But times had changed; nowadays it was the full-contact competitions that drew crowds. Few were interested in the old discipline of a traditional karateka. And who could blame them?

He sat for a while on the benches at Hasanabad Square until weekend crowds started emerging from the metro. Then he followed them to the junction of 30-Tir Street and Imam Khomeini Boulevard. They had recently cobblestoned this part of the city and set out food kiosks. Street musicians jammed the sidewalks, and a huge I ❤ TEHRAN neon sign shone off a wall of the Malek National Library. Hashem had loved going to all sorts of libraries when they were kids. He was also an avid book thief. For a long time the books he read went completely past Issa. One time on

Hashem's desk he'd seen a book titled *Of Mice and Men*. He was still in elementary school, and the title in Persian—*Moosh-haa va Adam-haa*—had really repulsed him. It seemed sinister to his young mind, even if he did not yet know what sinister was. He questioned the rationality of his brother's universe on these occasions. But he was also a soldier, there to defend Hashem, even if he did not quite know from whom and why. But as the years passed and Hashem's library expanded, he began to take a new interest in his brother's books, and their variety eventually became his own entry point into literature. By now theater had taken over Hashem's world. He was about to finish high school with dazzling grades, and their father could no longer force him into the dojo to humiliate him for loving an art form, as he had done with the violin. There was one book, Issa recalled, that never left his backpack: *Shakespeare Our Contemporary*. Issa thinking: *I know who Shakespeare is. We read about him in some class. But why "our contemporary"?* It seemed Hashem might always be trying to provoke their father with books out of the range of the old military man's understanding, and frankly Issa's understanding as well. It would take several years of studying at the university and fully catching up to Hashem's reading list before he began to get an inkling—a library with a shelf full of thin books by a man with hair like an eraser, Samuel Beckett; a book of poems by W. H. Auden, with the deeply lined face of a man whose gaze was a mixture of defiance and wisdom; and of course Hashem's film heroes with exotic, sexy, and excessively beautiful European names: Bresson, Pasolini, Fassbinder. "Look after my books," Hashem had asked him when he was finally leaving home. And he had, religiously, even getting a shelf built for them by hand. These were the very books that their father often thought of as the culprits stirring his firstborn toward that un-reachable place where only shame lay.

One day he'd come home to see the old man boxing all the books.

"*Pedar*, what are you doing?"

"I'm taking them to the bookshops along the university and selling them or giving them away. Maybe I'll throw them in the sewer. I don't know yet."

"But they're not yours to do that with."

The old man had looked up at Issa. "What did you say?"

"Those books are my *amanat*. They are in my care. A man has a duty not to betray an *amanat*. You know that."

"These books turned your brother *kooni*. You understand, son?"

"Books don't turn a person into one thing or another. And so what if they did? I've read most of those books by now. They're really mine."

"Yes, and I can tell you're turning into a homo like your brother."

It was the first time, and last, that in so many words he'd told his father to go fuck himself.

They remained there like two combatants. Issa stood his ground.

"I'm not betraying my brother like you betrayed your son."

The old man came at him then. His *yokogeri* side-thrust kick purposefully missing him by barely an inch but denting the wall with a loud boom. The old man could have crushed him. But Issa still did not budge. And the old man did not pursue the subject again.

The books stayed.

Three

I ssa woke up in the morning disoriented, unsure of his surroundings, suddenly recalling that, unlike Nasser who was a natural at sales—often simply bullying a customer into buying things they didn't need—he had not sold an expensive appliance in weeks. The owner of the Jomhuri store had warned him that going away to Beirut before Ramadan was as good as giving notice. Issa figured the guy was bluffing and would not fire him. And so what if he did? He could always pick up more classes to teach at the language institute.

A note sat in a breakfast tray next to him.

Tea on the stove. I am taking mother to the specialist.

Late the previous night he had walked from the I ❤ TEHRAN neon sign southward and then east toward the Grand Bazaar, finally arriving in the warren of narrow streets in Pamenar at an hour when the only people still outside were junkies and madmen. Aziz's home was in one of the dead ends where not much had changed in a half century, the area an odd mix of refurbished facades for the sake of nonexistent tourists and inner Pamenar itself, where the Jewish ghetto of Tehran had once flourished and then died.

Aziz, sturdy but tired, opened the door with, "You lost your way again, son?"

All Issa could do was to throw himself in her embrace, as if he were ten years old again and their father had brought her home only a month earlier—she, an Azeri Turk in need of an income, with a daughter Issa's age. At some point the old karate master got it into his head that it must be the absence of a woman that kept his son from being manly. His interesting logic brought him to the conclusion that if there was a woman in the house—and not just any woman but a "strong" woman, a sturdy Turk—then his son might finally come around.

Aziz was said to have beaten her deadbeat husband so thoroughly that the man hightailed it all the way to their native Iranian Azerbaijan and never looked back. She would either show up at the house early in the mornings before school or in the afternoons just after school. She cooked, cleaned, and did the laundry; but more importantly, she was a womanly presence with an iron hand, though the iron hand was mostly reserved for their father. When it looked like it would actually work out with her, the old man rented a nearby place for Aziz and her daughter, Solmaz. Both Hashem and Issa had taken to this redheaded Turkish woman immediately. In a neighborhood where hard-hitting men blustered down the main boulevard waiting for you to look crossly at their shadows, Aziz turned out to be a force of nature. The only time their father dared to get into it fiercely with Hashem was when Aziz was not around. Sometimes Issa wondered if the old man hadn't brought Aziz for just this purpose, as a way to check his own worst impulses. Once, after an especially brutal dressing-down that had taken place earlier in the day, Aziz had barged into the dojo just as class was about to begin.

"Make my son cry again and I will put a frying pan to your head, sir."

Issa pictured the old man like it was yesterday, standing in front of his disciples. This was the same man he had watched enter a gym in their neighborhood and ask for the bodybuilder who had called his son a sissy. When the mountain of a twentysomething-year-old appeared with a grin on his face, the old man proceeded to dismantle the guy limb by limb, making sure he would not even be able to go near a gym for another year and warning anybody who was there not to say a word to police or he would come back and break the rest of them. People believed him. He could and would do it. And yet here he was, with a grin of his own, watching a Turkish woman holding her long black *chador* between her teeth so that she could admonish him properly with her free hands, telling him he'd better lay off Hashem.

It was sublime.

All that the old man could say was, "He is not your son. He's mine."

"You don't deserve him, sir." The pronounced song of her accent leaving the old man, Issa, and the entire dojo with open jaws.

And something had indeed slowly begun to change for his brother with Aziz's arrival into their lives. The woman brought Hashem self-confidence. Not all the time, but enough so that Hashem could become his own person while the old man's occasional outbursts began to faze him less and less.

Somehow this unlikely Lorestani-Azeri Turk alliance—the two ethnicities that were the butt of every single joke in this cruel country—made it through several more years until it all went up in smoke.

He poured the tea and ate the tomato omelet they'd left for him on the tray. After the old man's death, Aziz had insisted on coming back here, to her old home in Pamenar. It was a poor person's version of a traditional Persian house with an inner courtyard, tiny and made mostly of earth and mud.

It was past noon. He didn't have a class to teach at the institute today, but the shift at Jomhuri began in two hours. He already knew he wouldn't be going.

After a while the creaky metal door opened and the two women came into the courtyard.

Aziz, her eyes as blue as the first day he'd laid eyes on her, said, "If you and Solmaz had gotten married, nothing would be different but everything."

She talked in riddles, and Issa sometimes wondered if it was processing her thoughts from Turkish into Persian that made her sound like a prophetess who could still threaten grown men with physical violence and mean it. Come to her door any afternoon and she might be feeding the scarecrow junkies of Pamenar slices of watermelon while chasing down the drug dealers with a broomstick or an oversize frying pan similar to the one she'd threatened their old man with, more than once, over the years.

An hour later, Solmaz was driving him to her practice in Baqershahr, near Tehran's sprawling main cemetery. They called her Madam Doctor. Patients lined up in the basement-turned-office that was attached to the local mosque. She charged a pittance for sick visits, unless people came to smooth their imaginary wrinkles or do laser hair removal, which in this ass end of town was as popular as anywhere but still a fraction of the cost of what it was in the northern districts of the city.

While she worked, Issa strolled around the area, just another beat-up part of the capital filled with Afghan refugees and people from the provinces who had come here searching forlornly for jobs. While overseas, he'd tried to forget that life mostly happened in thin doses of calamity in neighborhoods like this or over in Zam-zam, where Nasser lived. He'd foolishly followed news of home through sweeping canvases that always had to do with wars and revolutions in the Middle East. No one here really gave a fuck about revolution or war. Those things, he'd come to find out abroad, were only for academics and ax-to-grind exiles who never got tired of their own voices and lost riches. Here, the men who went across borders to fight and die, in one tired war after another, did so on their own account. And when they died, they were celebrated and grieved over for a minute. Then it was business as usual. What was that business? It was grown men coming to Solmaz's office to have the furrows in their foreheads filled because they worked as body washers at the cemetery down the road and wanted to get the stink of death off themselves when they went home. They wanted to look good. For their wives. For their girlfriends. For themselves. They wanted to belong to the living.

Madam Dr. Solmaz made those wishes real.

Solmaz would periodically have Issa come down to her office. She'd have him loiter about so people got to see she had a man in her life and didn't get any ideas. She did not introduce him as her husband but left it vague enough that people assumed it was either that, or he was her brother. Baqershahr was not somewhere you showed off a boyfriend, which he wasn't.

That evening after her shift, they sat in a jazz café in midtown near the university. A low saxophone came from the speakers, and young undergraduate students took turns at the piano and the drum set in the back room.

"He won't let me see my kid."

"He never intended to. Why are you bothered by it now, all of a sudden?"

"Because he's been coming around."

"What does he say? That if you agree to come back you'll be able to be with your kid again?"

"Something like that."

They sat there, as a brother and sister might. When Aziz and Solmaz had first joined their household and the old man realized Solmaz had never attended school, he'd confronted Aziz about it. Having been raised illiterate in her village, it had never dawned on Aziz that a girl could go to school. "She will get by without it, sir." But that wouldn't wash with the old man. The next day he took Solmaz to school himself and forced them to register her, even though she wasn't his daughter and had to start from first grade when kids her age were already in fourth.

The old man considered Solmaz his masterwork, and she worshipped him as much as she worshipped Hashem. She had thrived in school, and within a year and a half she was able to catch up and take the national elementary school exams with the rest of the girls her age. Several years later, she placed high enough in the countrywide college entrance exams that she qualified for medical school, all expenses paid by the state. Sometimes life was that way—an accidental hand came to lift you up from the unlikeliest place. Solmaz had turned out to be the old man's finest moment—the same man who destroyed his firstborn because he preferred the theater, violin, and men.

Issa asked, "How many women burn themselves in this country every year? Do you have any idea, Madam Doctor? I'm wondering about the statistics."

Solmaz eyed him as if they were twelve again and he'd hidden her shoes from her.

"It's a serious question I'm asking," he said.

"You know, Issa, you haven't been the same since you came back from America."

"I saw the world a bit." He gestured at the café and the street beyond it. "At least here no one pretends there is such a thing as justice."

"Oh, what a philosopher you've become. You need to get married."

"Look at where marriage got you!"

She went silent. He had hit a raw nerve. He remembered her first years at the university. Tall like her mother, with snowy Azeri skin, she had been approached more than once to model for the private, women-only fashion shows that were a part of Tehran's landscape then. They'd even approached her to become an actress and join the thriving film industry. But she'd have none of it. She was a bookworm and loved medicine. Her Achilles' heel, however, was her beauty. It was the same old story in this godforsaken place. Backbiting rumors ascribed everything she achieved to her having slept with this or that professor. Suitors lined up at Aziz's door, and she referred them to the old man who kept them at bay, until one day it was no longer possible. She had to get married and have

"taken" stamped on her forehead, so that the rumors would stop
and they'd leave her be. She was finishing medical school by then
and was considering specializing in dermatology. The day the old
man told him he'd said yes to a suitor, Issa had immediately asked,
"What about me?"

"She's your sister, you donkey."

He didn't know why all his life people had called him a donkey.
His ears were big, true. But Issa guessed there was probably something to it and he was really stupid in some fundamental way. At
least to his father he had been stupid, as the old man had never
forgiven him for reaching brown belt after years of karate practice
only to give it up rather than going for his black belt and becoming his natural successor at the dojo. Then, when Issa had gone
to university and signed up to study comparative literature rather
than something sensible like engineering or law, the old man at
last plain gave up on him and believed he had become a version of
his older brother.

"So have her marry Hashem," he'd said to the old man ear-
nestly, thinking that if it was a matter of just being married, both
Hashem's and Solmaz's reputations could be saved this way.

"Your brother is a woman. Donkey."

"Oh? So let one woman marry another."

"Shut your mouth. Both of you are a disgrace. Solmaz needs to
marry well. And that does not include a pair of losers like you and
your brother."

Issa hated him then, for just a moment. He'd done well with
his mandatory military service. By the time he was finishing high
school he could already destroy most black belts who'd started as
adults or even teenagers. When you practiced martial arts from

childhood, it stayed with you. Like bicycling. The color of the belt you'd reached meant nothing. You might lose a lot of your flexibility, your kicks may never reach as high as they once did, but unless you were facing someone who was just a plain animal that wouldn't go down, or was impossibly massive, or an expert, you could usually neutralize the adversary in the first few seconds of contact. They wouldn't know how to hit and you did; much more importantly, you were used to getting hit and they weren't. That was the bread and butter of any fight. At boot camp he'd shown them what he could do if he wanted to and it had paid off. He wanted to rub all this in the old man's face right then, but what good would come out of it? Solmaz was going to get married, she was tired, and she no longer seemed so averse to taking herself out of the running.

Then it happened. The "famous" doctor that she married turned out to be a lemon.

Were all men just shit, or was it that whoever had power—man or woman or child—would eventually use it? As a kid at the dojo, Issa was often given the job of leading the routine preliminary exercises for beginners. He would run those beginners to the ground, forcing them into long abdominal routines that broke men three, four times his size and age. He humiliated them until sometimes the old man himself had to intervene. It was a form of pleasure that came from having just that small bit of power you've been handed.

Solmaz's husband, a top eye surgeon and a university professor, would not allow her to go for her specialization, and after she became pregnant, he kept her from practicing medicine at all. It was just another husband-wife story waiting for someone like Nasser to come along and display his gallantry bullshit. But being a top eye surgeon also meant you had connections in the highest echelons of power. Half those corrupt bastards in the government were probably the man's patients. There was nothing Issa or anyone else could do about it. Nevertheless, Solmaz had fought back. And finally he gave her a divorce, with the stipulation that she would receive zero money from him and could only see her kid if and when he allowed it. It was a wonder he had even permitted her to get her private-practice license back. A couple of phone calls would have slammed those doors shut as well.

That was Solmaz's marriage in a nutshell. And in that jazz café in Tehran, Issa felt like telling her, *This is the world: you can either work the night shift in America and wait for your two-dollar tips, or you can stay here and shove Botox and facial cream in the cheeks of cadaver washers in a basement of a mosque complex next to the city's main cemetery.*

A young waitress brought them two very elaborate mint drinks. She smiled, chatting easily with Solmaz about her shifts that week. She was a university student, studying art and graphic design. Issa saw a longing in Solmaz's eyes as she smiled back and listened to the young woman. He thought he knew where this chat with the waitress had taken her. One day you're twenty and the world seems entirely possible. You are invincible and see things through the lens of prospects. A decade later it's as if you have been pushed to the back of the line and told to retreat until you disappear from the schematic of your own life. It doesn't matter if by then you've become a doctor or an asshole doctor's trophy wife.

He wanted to reach across the table and touch Solmaz through their combined discontent and offer her something more.

"Listen," he said when the waitress was gone, "I've made my decision. I'm going to sell the old dojo space. We can set you up a real practice uptown with just half the money I'll be getting for the place. I'll get a bigger apartment, too, and bring your mother to live with me."

Solmaz smiled. "My mother is glued to her old place. She won't leave. And I may as well be glued to that basement office by the cemetery. To build another practice in another part of town, it'll take years, Issa." She shrugged, "New patients, word of mouth, all that. I don't know, I just don't have the energy to start over again, you know?"

She drove them to the one-bedroom she'd been renting in the Yousef Abad district ever since her divorce. There was a *lavash* bakery directly underneath her house and the scent of freshly baked bread wafted into her kitchen and living room at all hours of the day and night. The grocer and the fruit and vegetable men consulted Madam Doctor about medicines and gave her discounts on their goods. It was a different world than Baqershahr here. A woman could live alone and the bother she received was more out of awe than predation.

On the way, he had asked her what she intended to do about the ex-husband. So far he only knew of her troubles through the lens of a volunteer who came down to Baqershahr once in a while so that Solmaz could keep the mosque men and the cadaver washers at a safe distance.

He took her silence about his question as meaning she was seriously considering going back to the surgeon. It would be an incarceration, like before. And because that was what it was, he knew that sooner or later he'd do something about it. He didn't know what just yet. It probably would be something as absurd as Nasser announcing there would be a fight in Zamzam because a woman had self-immolated. But what else could men like him and Nasser do? They were not lawyers. And even if they were, what good would it have done them here?

It was unlike Solmaz to pour them *arak* so late in the evening without even asking if he wanted some. Two shots in, she suddenly blurted, "I am going to fuck you tonight, Issa."

"Why do you say it like it's a death sentence?"

"Shut up. I'm serious."

"What, you are going to go back to that *koskesh* pimp husband of yours and you want to get a lick in before you go?"

She slapped him, reasonably hard. Like she used to do when they were kids.

He rubbed his face. "Hashem slapped me one time, just like this."

"You used to be a karate guy, Issa. You can take a slap."

Then she reached over and began kissing him for the first time in the nearly thirty years they'd known each other. Her lips didn't part, though. There was a coldness to it all, and he suddenly re-called Beirut and Arabic poetry, and, recoiling, pulled back.

"What? Get back into my mouth!"

"I was never in it. And what we're doing isn't right, Madam Doctor."

"Nothing is right, Issa. Do you know your brother and I tried to do it at least a dozen times when we were in high school? It never worked. He never could be hard for me."

"You loved him."

"I loved the idea of him. His intelligence mostly. I was stupid. I thought I could make him love women. You know why? Because I wanted it to be a favor to your father. I knew that was what he wanted. Your father wanted Hashem to be *turned* by a real woman. He never said it, but I knew that was what he wanted more than anything—for Hashem to become a man. He eventually gave up on the idea."

"I knew all this, Solmaz. I just never understood why you tried so hard to do this favor for my old man."

"I thought it was the one thing I could do to pay him back for all he'd done for me."

"What exactly did he do for you? He just registered you in school one day. That's it."

"You dumb donkey. That's everything. Where would I be today?"

"Where are you today?" he said a bit cruelly. "In Baqershahr, next to the cemetery?"

She slapped him again. And then pulled him close to kiss him. In minutes, their clothes were off in her bedroom.

"Bokon mano."

"No. You fuck me," he said. "Get on top and do what you need to do."

Halfway into it, he went limp. It felt like incest, and he knew she felt it too. Why were they doing this? As his wilted malfunction finally slipped out, making him hate himself and her and Hashem too for not being here with them, she remained on top of him and began punching and scratching. He let her, not even covering his face. And when she picked up a shoe from the base of the bed and continued, he still didn't move. They were soon both crying. They were again, maybe for the third or fourth time that day, ten years old, and eleven, and twelve, living in Monirieh and fighting over things kids fight over, and crying.

Back in the kitchen, keeping her face turned away from him, she asked, "You don't like women, same as Hashem?"

"You know I do."

"Then what happened just now?"

"You know that too. You are my sister."

She sighed and poured them another drink. "Last round."

He apologized.

"Did you ever do it with a man, Issa?"

"What does it matter? I'm not my brother, if that's what you want to know."

"I'm just curious. I want to know what that's like, is all."

"Just one time. When I was in New York. It was, I don't know . . ."

"What?"

He had never really told her about his life in New York. In fact, sometimes it seemed as if none of that life had ever happened. But it had, of course. He'd traveled to, and lived in, the one place everyone he'd gone to university with here dreamed of going to. And then he'd returned, a failure in people's eyes, as if going to that mythic city and not managing to stay was some sort of an offense. You could not explain to people why one chose to return. People had their own illusions, and a place like New York was on the list of every aspiring nobody who had seen *Taxi Driver* one too many times.

"I picked up a little habit over there, you know."

"Drugs?"

"I couldn't sleep."

As if the inability to sleep was an explanation for every flop that befell a person. He didn't say more for a while. Then he told her about going up to East 125th Street in Manhattan to get those doses of street methadone that kept him going during the day, so he could go to school and get a graduate degree—for no reason other than it was something to do. One of his last classes was on modernism. The usual suspects: Ezra Pound, Gertrude Stein, Picasso, Apollinaire, Kafka, interwar Paris, all that repetitious stuff of the last hundred years that he'd already inhaled in mostly mediocre Persian translation and at one time thought so dearly important. It had been a class taught by a man who bragged about his friendships with 1960s French film directors. He had thought of the guy as a harmless, even likable, charlatan, one who was no worse or better than anyone else he'd met in the hallways of an exodus life. All that had been before the police and those tiresome proceedings and threats of deportation. The only friendship in school had come with a ferociously handsome Pakistani classmate who knew English literature like an heirloom but would soon grow a beard a foot long, start wearing *kameez* tunics, and eventually disappear into the maw of fundamentalism somewhere between Karachi and Peshawar. But prior to losing his way, or finding it, he'd taken Issa to a bar on the Lower East Side of Manhattan. Before long, Issa was stone drunk and crying over the bar counter and into his empty beer glass. The Pakistani classmate was gone by then, and instead a stranger was offering him a tissue while Issa discoursed about Hashem.

"You've always been a crybaby, Issa," Solmaz offered.

"You're not exactly not one either."

"Go on."

"Nothing to go on. Me and the guy ended up in another part of town, called Brooklyn. His apartment. We kissed. I was drunk. Then I sucked his *kir* and drank his come."

"You did *what?*"

"It happens."

"How was it?"

"For about two days I felt satisfied with myself, as if I'd paid my debt to Hashem for not having understood him all those years. Afterward, for months and months, all I felt was guilt."

"Guilt for sleeping with a guy?"

"No, I didn't feel guilt over doing that. But for having done it for all the wrong reasons."

"So it was kind of like tonight, wasn't it?"

He asked her what she meant, but he already knew the answer. She said, "We had to try to sleep with each other at least once. I just don't know whom we were doing this for."

For Hashem, he would have said. But that wasn't it. Not entirely, anyway.

Just then an accordion player's music made its way to the intersection below them. It was late for street music. A neighbor began cursing the guy. When Issa went to the window and looked, another neighbor across the road was throwing cash from their second-floor balcony for the musician who seemed to know only one old song, "*Soltan e Qalbhaa*"—The Sultan of Hearts—which he played over and over again.

Four

He sat out the first half of the month of Ramadan and barely left the house. Rather than break the fast at sunset, he only drank water at night and slowly worked his way into fasting through a second sundown; it became a form of rapture, this hunger. His old man would tell the students at the dojo that pain was nourishment, as was hunger—though within reason. Ramadan was always a good excuse to center yourself if you'd been unsettled. And he did feel unsettled. The burned woman had done that to him, and that unconsummated fight over her in Zamzam, and the useless attempt at making love with Solmaz, not to mention the even more useless trip to Beirut for Maysa, the Arab poetess.

Fasting wasn't penance; it was recalibration.

In the meantime, the journal where Maysa's Arabic translations had been coming out seemed to have ceased operating, or else they'd been temporarily forced shut by the judiciary because of something they should not have published. Whatever it was, his trail on her had gone cold. He wrote several emails that went unanswered, and then the final time the email simply bounced back.

The elation from not eating made him giddy, almost an affliction. At the same time you could feel the trapped energy of the city waiting to break out each sunset, folks gorging themselves after another day's long fast. One night there was a knock on his door. He had just completed an extended bout of not eating. It was no longer about feeling weak or faint, but rather a lightness of being. As if losing touch with gravity.

He needed to eat.

As soon as he opened the door he knew what it was about. The *shahr-khar* had sent a couple of his guys on a strong-arm mission about the dojo space. Issa must have looked especially ghostlike that night, because one of them laughed and spoke to his partner as if Issa were barely there.

"This is the *gooz*? And his father was supposed to be some kind of karate master?" The man went into a mock kung fu movie stance and made a ridiculous and drawn-out *ooooo-ayaaa* sound.

Under normal circumstances maybe he would have let it go. But going that long voluntarily without eating lent you a recklessness. Reflexively, Issa crossed the threshold into the hallway in a side-stance and snapped a brutal *yokogeri*—the same side-kick that his old man had thrust into the wall that day he had wanted to give Hashem's books away—into the man's ribs. It was a clean kick. The kind of unhurried assault you perform on a heavy bag while two people hold it in place so that you can hammer your foot at a plain level into the bag's inner core. More of a show kick, really. But it had worked like a charm in this instance.

He felt the crack of the man's bone on the edge of his bare foot and watched him splay onto the wall in shock. The other man did not make a move. The suddenness of it all had overwhelmed all three of them. Without saying another word, he retreated inside and shut the door.

The next morning he packed a duffel bag and was on his way to the holy city, Mashhad, in the Khorasan province, by Afghanistan. There were several nights left till *Shab e Qadr*, the Night of Destiny, but Mashhad was already abuzz with pilgrims. Upon arriving, he slept most of the day at a pilgrim's hostel and spent from dusk until dawn by the shrine complex, watching throngs break their fasts and pray, then lingering as the vast courtyard slowly thinned out late at night and people went home to prepare to fast another day.

Nasser called incessantly, at last sending a photo of the inside of Issa's apartment. The place looked worked over a bit.

"You mean you are inside my apartment now?" Issa said after finally picking up.

"No, not right now."

Then Nasser began talking fast. But Issa drifted, losing the thread of their phone conversation. He had stopped going to the sales job on Jomhuri Avenue altogether, and the new school term at the language institute would not begin until after Ramadan. He'd tried calling Solmaz a couple of times after that night, but she would not answer. She must have felt something of the shame he felt—not for trying to sleep with each other, but for failing miserably at it. If at least they'd succeeded, maybe there would have been a measure of relief in their transgression. But they didn't even have that. And now, for all he knew, she was probably back with her ex-husband. He'd seldom asked about the son she'd had with the surgeon. Once, she had shown him a photograph. The kid looked intelligent and was a little chubby. By the time she was pregnant with him, Issa was already on his way to America, and by the time he'd come back, the boy was already nearing adolescence. He was not that naïve to imagine a mother could simply shed herself of her child, even from a forced marriage, but he wondered if having been forced might at least make it just a little bit easier. He doubted it.

Hell, there were infinite reasons why a woman, or a man, would burn themselves. And ever since that night when he and Nasser had had the near fight over the self-immolated wife, he walked around trying to guess who on the streets of this country was desperate enough to want to do such a thing to themselves. What final bump of bad luck could push that person past the edge.

Over the phone, Nasser was saying, "Where are you right now, Issa? Did you go to Beirut again looking for someone to love?"

"I'm in Mashhad actually. At the shrine."

"They've gone through your place. Not too badly, though. I think they just wanted you to know they were here. Do you hear me? You weren't answering your phone, so I came by. They broke your door lock."

"It doesn't matter. I have nothing worth taking anyway. Just some books."

"Well, the books are still there. Was it the *shahr-khar*?"

"Who else?"

He told Nasser about what had happened and the hurt he'd laid on one of Haj Davood's men. Nasser laughed, obviously pleased to hear Issa had cracked someone's rib.

"Please just have my lock fixed, and I'll take care of the rest once I get back."

"What? You're going to go into Haj Davood's office and pick a fight with everyone there? I'll come with you, then."

"No, brother. I'm not like you. I don't pick fights in my own neighborhood if I can help it."

"But you just did."

The cool night breeze seemed to buoy the entire shrine complex just then. If Khoda was anywhere, it was here; a nearby worshipper was uttering Allah's many names in their prayers, just loud enough that Issa could hear.

Nasser said, "I need you back. Please. The past three weeks, my mother has found three women for me to marry. She's even gone and talked to one of the families. I don't want to get married, Issa."

"Why not?"

"Because I guess I am a donkey, too, like you, and I need to feel love first."

"Nasser."

"What?"

He took a deep breath. "I have a sister. A sort of sister. You can, well, maybe marry her."

Nasser grumbled. "You're not taking me seriously."

"Listen to me. She's a Madam Doctor." As if being a Madam Doctor explained everything. He wasn't really sure what he was saying or offering to Nasser, and whether Solmaz would think him an idiot for it. But being at the shrine he felt inspired. Either this was an elegant solution to several problems, or it was more of his donkey ways.

He hung up before Nasser could decline the offer.

What anguish on my account can he endure if he has not seen me?
What anguish if he has?

Maysa, the woman he didn't find in Beirut, had translated those words. He thought he could reach across time and that thousand-year-old obscure mystical Arabic text and find her at last—beyond the pages of transient Persian literary journals. If only he could pray hard enough or long enough, or if he fasted well past the duration of the month of Ramadan. Something surely had to give.

HIS NAME WAS JAFAR. They had come up through the ranks at the dojo together. A half decade older, Jafar had been just old enough to run away from home and volunteer toward the end of the long war of the eighties as a teenage fighter. He was the only person Issa had stayed in contact with after leaving for America. But Jafar had also done what Issa would do three years later and given up the practice once he was a seasoned brown belt, though he could have easily gone for black. There was something at once sacrilegious and profound about giving up the practice when you were so close to the much-coveted terminal color. It was not un-like giving up on life itself. It took a special nihilism, arriving at a place where you realized everything you ever did and would do was dust and of no consequence. Black, white, all the colors in between, nothing mattered.

So when Issa did what Jafar had already done and quit karate, the first thing the old man had to say to him was, "You are doing a Jafar. Why?"

He figured, why not? He wanted the life Jafar had. Jafar had returned to his ancestral home of Mashhad. Soon, camera in hand, the onetime teenage soldier was across the border in Afghanistan joining the Northern Alliance under the legendary commander Ahmad Shah Massoud, fighting the Taliban fundamentalists. Once in a while, when Jafar came to Tehran, they'd meet far away from the dojo, Issa barely out of his late teens and still marginally bound to the practice, while Jafar was already doing all the things war junkies like him dreamed of. He had begun to sell combat footage to television channels. The stories he told of the Northern Alliance fighters made Issa dream of real combat in distant places, rather than doing mind-numbing sentry duty in some out-of-time garrison for his looming army stint.

It was a few years later—after Ahmad Shah Massoud was assassinated—that Jafar's life blew apart. And in a way, so did Issa's. All that time, he had imagined he'd someday be joining Jafar and the Northern Alliance; they'd be among the great Massoud's intimates, fighting the good fight against religious zealots. At night, they'd sit around campfires with the commander par excellence, discussing Persian poetry and believing themselves warriors, far from the chicken crumbs of everyday life.

It was all romantic nonsense, and Issa knew being around a guy like Massoud didn't help to clear your head. Jafar had told him that one time, in the midst of battle, he and the commander had been discussing the rare ghazals of a magnificent Persian poetess who had died far too young. Massoud's lieutenant kept popping into the tent to say the battle was heating up, and maybe he should stop discussing Persian poetry just then and get on with the business at hand.

We do all this fighting, for the sake of the writing.

Massoud's response to his lieutenant, which rhymed in Persian, to this day made Issa wonder what it was that made women and men do the things they did and go to the places they went—people like himself, or Jafar, who, not long after Massoud's assassination, had been badly injured during a raid. Not exactly disabled but having to live with a lifetime of physical pain, Jafar had taken refuge in meds, just as Issa had taken refuge in methadone and anxiety pills. Two combatants fallen from grace, has-beens of the martial way of life who never arrived at that black belt.

"Issa, you look like the angel of death has visited you."

Jafar lived in the outskirts of Mashhad, in a cul-de-sac often visited by old Afghan vets he'd served with back in the day. The basement of his house was divided into small rooms where other vets, coming nowadays from places like Iraq and Syria, stayed. Issa had seen this other group of soldiers in Tehran, too, especially in Monirieh, men who were lost to the commerce of peace and did not know what to do with themselves in the intervals they came home to rest, their lives suspended until they returned to their various theaters of combat.

He told Jafar about hurting one of the men the *shahr-khar* had sent and the going-over his apartment had received afterward.

"So you're here to hide?"

Now that he thought about it, he wasn't sure why he'd come. He'd known Jafar almost as long as he'd known Solmaz and Aziz. Jafar had always been there, at the dojo, practicing. Until he wasn't. After his Afghan years, he had settled down to write op-eds for several conservative newspapers. He was an insider, and because of his past he had friends in high places in intelligence and was their go-to man when they needed advice on Central Asia and Kabul.

"I'm here just to see you, old friend. You're still a bachelor."

Jafar laughed. "Am I good for anything else?"

"I thought your brother and his family were living with you."

"Gone to the ancestral village for Ramadan." Jafar pointed to the basement. "These other young brothers will head back to some war or another after the month is up, then the family returns."

"Why?"

"Why do I host my brother and his family? Or why do I host the fighters?"

"Both."

"Because I'm an old soldier with a destroyed body, Issa. It gets lonely here."

"Marry, then."

"So a young wife from the village can help me to the toilet every time I have to go?"

"People marry for all kinds of reasons."

While they talked, Issa could hear the footsteps of the vets going back and forth to the kitchen, making tea, speaking in low voices to one another. They were ghosts, careful not to impose on their host, and acting as if they already had one foot in the other world, on leave from war only to negotiate the terms of their own imminent end.

Issa said, "I guess I'm really here to ask you what I should do with the dojo. You're the only person I know who understands what that place means to me. It's my inheritance."

"It may be your inheritance, but it stopped being a dojo once your father, may Khoda have mercy on his soul, passed. Sell it.

You are living in a purgatory, Issa. This is why you got up and went to the West. What did you think was waiting for you over there?"

Since it was a special occasion, Jafar prepared a *bast* of opium for them over a charcoal brazier. Issa took a long, sweet inhalation, the elegant scent of the thing wafting across the empty room and sinking into the cushions and pillows around them.

What did he think was waiting for him there? Escape. He repeated the story that Jafar only vaguely knew—how after the old man's and Hashem's deaths all he'd wanted to do was run away. On a lark, he'd paid the application fee to enter the annual immigration lottery the Americans offered. Maybe one chance in a million to win, and he'd won. He did not know how to explain to Jafar that he had to give the West and its promise of something better a try. You don't win the raffle and then simply throw away the ticket.

Or maybe you do—or should.

He hadn't. And he wasn't sorry about it, even when he realized that life there, too, was mostly quiet desperation.

"Jafar, those last two years of my brother's life were hell. I brought him back to the old place after our father died. He was sick by then. I took care of him day and night."

"I know you did."

"What you don't know is how it feels taking care of someone who is terminally ill. It's a death sentence, and not just for the patient."

"I've seen a lot of death, Issa." Jafar made a gesture toward his own legs with the opium pipe. "The only reason I'm sitting here with you today is because I, too, won a lottery of sorts. Four out of five people in my military convoy were killed." He sighed. "I wish I had been too."

"Don't talk that way. Marry instead, brother. I'm serious. Find yourself a good someone. Have a child or two. It's not too late."

"And pass on my bitterness to a wife and child? A child deserves life, Issa. Not some dried-up shadow for a father. My brother and his family, sure, they stay here. But they know nothing of my life. Nothing. They don't even ask how I was injured all those years ago. I'm a ghost, frightening and dreary. I keep to myself, even in my own house. I prefer it that way. A man who knows time is never on our side is a man one step ahead of the fool who doesn't even know that much."

"Then why go to Afghanistan when you did? Why fight? Why do any of the things you did back then?"

"I was misinformed."

"By whom?"

"Mostly by poetry."

They sat there quietly, measuring the arcs of their reduced lives. Issa had once tried explaining to Solmaz that the worst part of taking care of someone with an illness like AIDS was when they actually had a good day and were less sick. On those days, Hashem would suddenly want to leave the house and see sunlight again. It was fleeting, and inevitably he'd be twice as sick the next day. And it was devastating to watch. But Solmaz would have none of it. She saw things through the lens of a physician. She wanted to save her own childhood soul mate any way she could, whereas Issa wanted Hashem to die quickly and without more suffering. On one of the days Hashem had felt better, he'd left the house while

Issa was out. An hour or two later he was dead. Thrown to the ground on a side street. Nothing taken. The police report said the blunt strike to the head was hardly one that would kill a man. "It was just that your brother was . . . well, you know, not very healthy. They—the perpetrators—probably just meant to push him around a little."

They? How did the cop know they were more than one? And pushing him around just a little meant what exactly?

After that day, and until the day he'd won the American lottery and left, he thought of all of Monirieh as the perpetrator. The neighborhood itself, that fetid ethos and its ways. Solmaz, in a moment of cruelty and anger at him, had said, "You're happy now, aren't you? You wanted your brother gone." It was the most punishing thing she would ever say to him.

But was it the "blunt strike" that had ultimately killed Hashem, or was it the disease? If only one could measure the allotments of horror with some precision.

He asked Jafar, "How did it feel, the day you heard the news they'd assassinated your hero, Ahmad Shah Massoud?"

Jafar eyed him for a while in silence.

"It was a moment. One distinct moment. I mean, there was the moment before the news and the moment after. Life stopped for a minute. And then I had to change the scaffolding of my mind. Or I would lose it."

"Then you understand what I went through after Hashem died."

Jafar frowned. "What do I understand, Issa?"

"Why I had to leave for America. I, too, had to change the

scaffolding of my brain after my brother's death. At least for a while I did."

"Sell the dojo, Issa."

THE NEXT MORNING before going to the airport for his return flight, Issa stopped by the shrine for the last time to say a prayer. He saw it then. On the bottom rack of a magazine kiosk just a ten-minute walk from the shrine sat a volume of an obscure journal he hadn't seen before. He bought it just to have something to read on the plane. Maysa's translation from Arabic was on page 76:

Stooped and deformed, all letters are consumed by sickness, save for the upright Aleph which stands erect and tall.

He reread the lines she'd published in that journal all the way to Tehran. It was true, the aleph—the first letter of the Arabic alphabet—did stand upright. Whereas the other letters were curved and stooped. But what of it? It was as if the poet or translator or whatever she was had meant to send him on another wild-goose chase around the Levant.

The first thing he did the next day, though it was Ramadan, was to visit the offices of the journal, a one-room operation off a side street near Valiasr Square. It turned out they were in fact running several journals from there and were probably making a slim profit in the black market off the difference in cost between the paper they purchased at government quotas and what they actually used. As surprised as he was to find them there in the heat of Ramadan, they were just as astonished to see an actual visitor to their operation. Without much fuss at all, they gave up the email address of the translator/poet who had sent them the submission and threw in a couple of extra issues of the journal as a thank-you.

Issa banked Maysa's new address in his to-do list and went about cleaning up the mess in his apartment that the *shahr-khar*'s men had left behind. That night, he decided to pay the *shahr-khar* a visit. It was the first of the Nights of Destiny. Haj Davood's usually crowded real estate office was empty, only him and two old emphysemic-looking guys. None of his bodybuilders were around. It would have been easy to raise the volume on their dispute. But what would be the point of that? Haj Davood wanted to buy the dojo and Issa wanted to sell it.

"Let us come to an understanding and not disrespect each other anymore. I'm a seller, you're a buyer. Let's make it happen. At a reasonable price."

Haj Davood grunted but seemed accommodating for a change. "Done."

Five

"Ramadan is over, son," Aziz said, moving aside to let Issa into her courtyard, "but you are not looking strong. Your father would not be happy." She hobbled to the stove and put on tea.

Issa had been keeping to his apartment, continuing to fast well past the month and making daily phone calls to Solmaz that had gone unanswered.

An hour after arriving at Aziz's, he was still complaining to her about Solmaz when there was a knock at the door.

"Your sister is making a decision, son. I gave my daughter to a bad man. Actually, it was your father who gave her away. I should not have let him."

"You didn't know better, Nana."

Aziz, whom all of Monirieh used to call Aziz Turkè as a term of endearment for a woman with what was really a man's name, put on her hijab and shuffled to the courtyard to answer the knock. When Issa had arrived earlier, the usual druggies were busy working themselves into the evening high. Now he heard one of them at the door, asking Aziz for sugar cubes to take with their tea. Aziz's voice from the shadows swore some old familiar Turkish curses that essentially told the man he was the father or son of a dog and that if he did not stop taking drugs she would send him where she had sent that no-good husband of hers years ago. Issa brought the cubes to Aziz, who gave them to the thin man and his thin company. She cursed the whole lot of them and slammed the door shut.

She sighed. "The bad man has given my daughter one week to be with her own boy. He has evil inside of him. I don't care if he is a doctor—I am sure he is a bad one."

"Solmaz gets to keep her son for a week?"

They stood in that tiny earth-and-mud yard, the jubilant night sounds of post-Ramadan mixing with the eagerness of the men outside, whose lives were conditioned by habit. He had at one time gone to the edge of this world of theirs and managed to pull himself back. Barely.

"One week is all he gives her. I told her not to take the boy. Not for one week, not for one day. Nothing. It is a trap, son. One week for a woman to be a mother again. Then he takes the boy away, and what next? Next he will say to her: 'If you want to spend more time with your boy you must come back to the marriage.'" Aziz let out a deep breath. "Khoda bless you, son, but the evil of men has no end. Sons of dogs, all of you. Except for your poor late brother. To Khoda we belong and to Him we return."

"Nana, do you want me to do something about the doctor?"

Aziz regarded him in the semidarkness. Often, he had wondered what this woman would have become had the accident of birth brought her into the world somewhere other than her native Maragheh.

"Son, do not allow my daughter to go back to that marriage."

He nodded.

"She wanted to bring the boy here, but I told her no. I told her I don't want to see your boy."

"You don't want to see your grandson?"

"Once I feel that love, I am finished. Khoda will strike me. I cannot see the boy again after so long. Solmaz is angry at me, but I will not have it."

"You have nerves of steel, Nana."

She looked at him for another moment, and then she seemed to have a lump in her throat. He did not remember another time when Aziz Turkè had looked so broken, not even when Hashem died. It shook him. She muttered quietly to herself, in her heavily accented eastern Turkish, things Issa didn't understand.

"Khoda have mercy on his soul," she then said as she opened the front door again.

"On whose soul, Nana?"

"Your late brother. Who else?" She pointed to a half dozen Persian melons sitting by the side of the door. "Hand one to me." He did. She called over the same guy she had threatened to beat up a few minutes ago and handed him the melon. "Take it and go away," she barked in Turkish.

The door remained open. Issa waited.

"One time, I came to the house and found your brother with a boy. They were . . . may Khoda strike me twice dead. I was about to slap your brother and that boy, but then we heard your father coming into the apartment. Do you know what I did? I pretended the boy was my nephew. I don't know if your father believed me. I think not." She was silent for a minute. "I don't want to lose more people to this world, Issa. I want to go before you and Solmaz. I don't want Solmaz to go back to that bad man. And I don't want to see again the boy she had with him."

"Nana, the boy is your grandson."

"All the more reason. There are things you cannot understand. You are not in my place."

He had to ask. "Nana, why did you want to slap Hashem?"

She shook her head and started to walk away, leaving him by the open door.

"I thought I could save him. I don't know. I thought . . ." She didn't finish.

"It's all right, Nana."

"Nothing is all right. Nothing. I miss your brother. Maybe I should have slapped him. No. I did right. He was my boy. Like you are my boy. I don't want another boy. I don't want to see Solmaz's boy. I don't have enough room in my heart." She struck at her chest. "You understand? This heart is full. No more room for anyone." He was about to say that he understood, but she carried on. "Issa, now you will tell me this: 'I understand, Nana.' But you understand nothing, son. You went away all these years and now you come back to tell me what?"

"I am sorry, Nana, that I went away. I was confused."

"You were. I don't blame you. Now go home. On your way out, give those fools in the alley another melon."

MAYSA WROTE HIM BACK an email: *Grief on my account is grief's essence.*

He wrote her back asking for the original Arabic sentence to her translation. She sent it. And then he argued with her that she was misusing the word *essence*, whereas what the translation really required was the word *truth*.

He was being petty. He had wavered a few days before writing to her new email address. More days passed; the Fitr celebration of the end of the month of fasting had long since come and gone. The city was alive again in the worst possible way—heat, traffic, short tempers. In the email he'd written about her "Aleph" translation: *You know, I feel like those "stooped and deformed" letters of the alphabet that you write about. Why send me on a pointless chase to Beirut when you don't live there?*

She replied, *I stand with him whose burden I've become, even if he turns away from me.*

He decided to leave it alone. No more writing to Maysa.

With the fasting month finished, Nasser forced Issa to go with him to his hometown, about two hours' drive southeast of Tehran, so that he could get a look at the "suitable women" his family had found for him. Issa had never been on this kind of outing and felt like a busybody trapped in a time warp. He knew that Nasser felt exactly the same, which was why he wanted Issa along. Nasser's family was hardly pleased with Issa's presence. But Nasser insisted.

Two weeks and four suitable brides later, all of them rejections from Nasser's end, and they were done. Nasser's family refused to have Issa accompany him to meet any more potential matches, and Nasser, in turn, refused to marry at all. The whole thing had been a farce so that Nasser could tell his family he had given it a shot and hadn't found what he was looking for.

On their long drive back from the last matchmaking session,

Issa brought up Solmaz. "Now are you ready to meet my sister, the Madam Doctor?"

"I'm not stupid. You don't have a sister."

"You know what I mean."

"A suitable doctor."

"Yes, Solmaz is a *very* suitable doctor."

"How is she suitable?"

Issa gave a quick rundown of Solmaz's life—the surgeon she'd married, the divorce, not being allowed to see her kid, and Issa's worry that she was going to go back to the guy. Nasser didn't seem moved or pleased about the proposal. Trouble clouded his face.

"Nasser, what's eating you?"

"Everything. Have you even asked Madam Doctor about your proposal?"

"No."

"So you're no better than all these fools who want to marry people off."

"I want to do right by a woman who is like a sister to me."

"Did you bother to think for a minute what I might want or what Madam Doctor might want?"

"I was just trying—"

Nasser didn't let him finish. "Who are you to make these decisions?"

They'd been cruising along, but now, when a spanking new BMW came to overtake them on the left lane, Nasser suddenly hit the gas and started going neck and neck with the driver at high speed. In the passenger seat was a young woman who looked through the window at them as if she were looking at wild animals. Fear was all over her face, while the man appeared frozen, not taking his eyes off the road in front of him. Nasser drew to within inches of them, honking his horn and looking like a mad bulldog. This wasn't the first time he had inflicted road rage with Issa in the passenger seat. No one ever challenged him. One look and you knew it wouldn't be a good idea.

Now he rolled the window down and screamed into the wind, "Rich fucks!"

"Enough!" Issa shouted.

It was out of character for Nasser to obey but he did, slowing down and letting the other car go on its way.

"Why did you have to humiliate that poor guy like that?"

"Because I'm angry."

"At what?"

"I don't want to get married. Not to anyone from my town and not to your *jende* of a Madam Doctor."

"Call my sister a whore again and you'll have to fight me. I mean it."

"I'm sorry. I just don't want to be married."

"Fine. You don't have to scare people to death on the highway for that."

Then they both shut up until they reached Issa's place. In no time, Nasser had downed a half bottle of strong *arak* while pulling random books off Issa's shelves.

"Did the *shahr-khar* make an offer yet?" he asked.

"I've told him he has to buy my apartment too. And give it all in cash at once."

"You want out of Monirieh, don't you?"

Issa nodded. "Too many ghosts."

The *arak* laid Nasser low at last. He sat on the couch and eyed the ceiling. "Are you telling me this *mahal*, Monirieh, killed your brother?"

"No, our *mahal* didn't kill him on purpose. But its inhabitants didn't let him live an easy life either."

"That's killing a person if you ask me."

"I don't disagree."

"This whole business of marriage, my father says he'll disinherit me if I don't get married. I told him to go to hell. You?"

"What about me?"

"Your Beirut beloved. What came of that?"

"A dead end. Finished."

"Ah. Lucky man." Nasser set down his *arak* next to the couch. "You know what fire is, Issa? You don't know hot until you've seen a building that starts to melt in front of you. That kind of hot. It's the devil itself. Men, women, everybody—we're just a building burning together, you know."

Six

I t started on the first day of the new term at the language institute. A conversation class for people who were hoping to emigrate to English-speaking countries like Australia or Canada.
Fifteen alert and hopeful students, men and women, raising their
hands dutifully and asking questions at every turn. They'd already been told at registration that their instructor had lived a
long time in the United States, so they looked upon Issa with awe.
Who had the heart to tell them mostly drudgery awaited them
wherever it was they were going? His job here was a lie, he knew.
But language wasn't a lie; he did what he could.

After the class, one of the students in the back row came up to
him. He had a glossy black ponytail and wore a tight, mesh-like
sleeveless black top that clearly defined his slim upper body. He
smiled broadly. To Issa, he was beautiful in the way that many of
Hashem's theater people had been beautiful, a certain exquisite
androgynous core that assaulted you and then made you surrender
during their underground performances. It took a few beats before

Issa recalled that affectionate smile from years earlier. He hadn't been one of Hashem's main actors, but part of an extended family of actors and actresses that had always hung around.

"It's Mehran. You remember me?"

"Of course I do."

Some sixteen years ago, Mehran had been a boy just out of high school. Hashem's plays, never mainstream but with a cult following that packed the house every night, were always filled with extras who simply wanted to be in the orbit of that world. Hashem was the "sick, gay, boy wonder" who was changing the staid landscape of theater here, and to be a part of his crew was to no longer be an outcast in a country that forbade and punished so many things big and small. Issa had been the younger brother who visited now and then, not speaking all that often to Hashem's people, because at the time he wanted to believe he did not relate. Or maybe because in his own seasick mind—coming right out of the cracks and sidewalks of Monirieh—he attributed Hashem's worsening illness to the path his older brother had chosen for himself. It had been thick armor that Issa wore, allowing him to imagine that by staying put and ramrod straight he could somehow save his brother from the virus.

He hadn't saved a bloody thing.

Mehran pulled up a chair close to the teacher's desk and sat. He reached and held Issa's wrist. Issa didn't flinch, surprising himself.

"Your brother, he was our hero. You know that."

"I know."

"We heard you'd gone away, Issa."

"I did go away. I came back."

"But why?"

Mehran had asked the question with an undertone of outrage in it. *Who the fuck comes back here?* he was really asking.

"It didn't work out for me. That's all."

Moments passed and mostly Mehran just kept staring into Issa's eyes in disbelief. It was awkward at first. Issa tried making small talk. Why take this class? Where did Mehran intend to try emigrating to and why? Mehran answered all the questions obediently, talking about how hard it was to make a living here, how he got harassed all the time for the way he looked, how he wasn't sure where he'd apply for asylum but he was sure to try. He wore a pair of drop-shaped ruby earrings, had on a hint of an eyeliner, and his eyebrows were neatly plucked. His soft, hairless skin did not have the slightest trace of years on them. He had to be in his midthirties now, and if anything, time had only matured the earlier imprecision of his gender in the decade and a half that had passed. Issa sat there thinking: *This is a striking-looking person.* He checked himself, felt uncomfortable, but then let go of the discomfort and relaxed a bit, letting Mehran speak.

Mehran continued smiling at him. "Issa, you really don't remember, do you?"

Issa shifted in his chair. "Remember what?"

"The week you and I spent together."

"I . . ."

"No, I don't mean it like that."

He remembered. Of course he remembered. It hadn't been just Mehran, though, but a coterie of Hashem's youngest actors. They'd taken him around, shown him life beyond their theater world because he'd finally asked them to. He wanted to know, he'd told them. *What do you want to know, Issa? We're not animals in a zoo, you realize?* Why would they say that to him, even if they only said it in jest? And why was it always so difficult to get anything right in this world? Someone was always taking offense, he thought, and just because he didn't yet have the language to say the right things.

One day during that week Mehran had said, *And what if I were to kiss you? I'd like to.* Issa saying nothing. Clamming up. Remembering that time in school when he'd smashed that poor kid for doing exactly that, kissing him. Even now, sitting right here in this classroom, he realized he had been pretending to himself that he didn't know Mehran as well as he did. Why had he done this? What kind of dismal psychology lay behind all that? And why didn't all the books he'd read—his own and Hashem's—lend an iota of advantage at moments like this?

Because books could not live your life for you. That's why.

Toward the end of that week, in one of the restaurants near the university, he'd noticed a group of his classmates walking through the door while he sat with Mehran and three other actors. He had wanted to melt into his seat and become invisible. Mehran caught the change in him right away and called him out on it. *You're not committing a crime sitting at this table with us, Issa* jaan. He'd felt like the shit he was at that instant—embarrassed at being embarrassed. Then he was angry—at the world, at those classmates for coming in there; he was angry at Hashem's illness, and he was angry with Hashem for being ill at all.

He mumbled, "I remember, Mehran *jaan*. I remember that week together. How could I forget?"

"Then how come you acted like you didn't know me today in class until I came up to you?"

"Sounds like an interrogation."

"I'm just curious. I want to know if I'm still talking to the same Issa, or if you became somebody else."

"I'm still the same Issa. And I didn't notice you because this was the first day of class, there were fourteen other students in there, and nearly as many years had passed."

"It's all right. I believe you."

He wanted to say, *I'm not sure if I believe it myself.* But he stayed silent, as did Mehran. The past was a wasteland that sat between them. Because it wasn't just Hashem who had died of the disease. There had been others. Many others. Ephemeral young men whose lives and deaths no one besides their theater companions really wanted to acknowledge, least of all their own families.

"Issa, after your brother died, we were all like orphans. The whole troupe. Everyone. We didn't know what to do with ourselves. Hashem had a way with him, even in sickness, even till those last years when you came and took him home with you. He was a work-aholic, you know. He kept us working, hoping. We put on shows that had to be whispered about. We couldn't advertise them in those days. They would have hauled us all to jail. But we were all happy. And then, suddenly, all of it was gone in a moment."

Was Mehran going to tear up? No, he held himself together, his voice unwavering, and then he brightened up again. "You have to come see us, Issa."

"Where?"

"Anywhere. It's not like the old days. We put on shows in real theaters now. Not crazy stuff like your brother used to do. But stuff they won't shut us down for."

Issa laughed. "Oh, so you all became tame?"

"Age, my love. Age and, well, one has to make a living."

Just then, the door opened. A class was waiting to come in, and the manager of the place stuck his head in, saw them sitting there practically holding hands, and retreated as if he'd been electrocuted.

Mehran laughed and made a face. "I think I just got you in trouble."

"No, you didn't."

THAT THURSDAY EVENING, Issa and Nasser stood in line outside of a theater on one of the side streets next to Daneshjoo Park. It was the start of the weekend, and the line was very long. It didn't look like they would get seats. Just then, Mehran peeked outside, noticed them, and gestured for them to cut through the queue and come in.

At first, Issa had been worried Nasser would give him a hard time about this place. Maybe he'd even get violent. It was not impossible. The city's *roshan-fekr* crowd was here in abundance, the so-called enlightened minds: the writers and journalists, the theatergoers and art students, the musicians, actors, and painters, café society and their interesting hair and ambiguous sexuality. It was a far cry from the Zamzam district where Nasser lived, and even more so from Monirieh and the dojo and the weight-lifting gyms. It was Hashem's world of casual commitments and relativity in the heart of the Islamic Republic.

Issa prepared himself for the worst when Mehran kissed him on the cheeks. Next, extending a soft hand for Nasser to shake, Mehran looked into Nasser's eyes, smiled, and asked, "Who is this handsome, hard-looking man you brought along?"

Before Issa could speak, Nasser took Mehran's hand, smiled back, and said, "This hard man is Mr. Nasser of the Zamzam district. If there is a fire, I'll put it out."

There was a pause. And then, softly, Mehran said, "What if you are the fire, Mr. Nasser?"

"Then I guess someone will have to lend me a hand."

That may have been the moment Nasser surpassed his world of Zamzam and everything he'd known until then. It was as if he were a different man. Capable of irony and flirtation, and at a decibel Issa would have never foreseen in him. What Issa saw was Nasser taking one look around at a crowd that was alien to him, at a place called a theater, to which he had never been before, and to a man who had on earrings and faint pink lipstick—this fire captain, this tough guy of Zamzam, the man who took your revenge for you whether you asked for it or not—and making a sudden, startling adjustment. Issa was shocked. And this shock stayed with him throughout the night as they were ushered by Mehran into the hall and given the best seats in the house.

The play turned out to be a messy version of *King Lear* told from the daughters' perspective. It took him back to his first year of college. Hashem was long gone from home, already making his name in the art scene that had slowly reemerged after the revolution. Hashem was living in a dilapidated brick building on Henri Corbin Street that had existed before the area became fashionable again and the old building was turned into a café and gallery. Issa would visit him there, and Hashem would talk to him about Shakespeare and the philosophy of the medieval Persian mystic Suhrawardi in one breath. Issa didn't understand it all just yet, but he thought he was getting there—closer to his brother's world. Their old man was never mentioned, not once. Both already knew Hashem had the virus, but rather than taking proper drugs, which were available, Hashem had opted for some kind of bullshit meatless odyssey and traditional Persian and Chinese medicines, which involved a lot of herbs and extracts and teas. He wasn't sick yet, but Issa could feel him getting lighter every time they met. When Hashem caught colds it took forever for him to recover, yet he persisted with his meatlessness and herbs. Issa was enraged with him, as was Solmaz. But they could do nothing about it. It was during that time that Hashem staged his Persian take on *King Lear* that became the talk of the Tehran underground, a brutal and bloody three-hour-long affair that was finally shut down by the authorities for no other reason than because they could. Issa remembered coming out of that play with Solmaz feeling like they'd been punched in the gut, their foundations shaken.

So many years later, seeing another *King Lear* with Nasser sitting next to him, his attention wouldn't hold. This version of the old king and his daughters was thin at best. Mehran played the part of one of the two evil daughters; he did a fair job, overacting on purpose with even more luster than a half hour ago. Issa couldn't quite figure out if he was Goneril or Regan in the play, and it didn't really matter. But he noticed that Nasser's eyes were fixed. At one point, Issa elbowed him and joked that had he known Nasser would love theater this much he would have brought him along earlier. Nasser didn't answer but stayed focused and serious.

Before long the audience stood up and was clapping. This town had changed so much in the years Issa wasn't here. Nowadays, every other theater troupe got invitations to go to Europe and perform.

You could actually make a living off this life even if you were not very good at it. Europeans didn't mind parting with their money for art, and especially if it meant helping the wretched of the earth. Besides, their euros went a long way here. It hadn't been like this at all when Hashem was alive. Once again, Issa could not help but rue lost time and bad luck. Why did Hashem have to go so early? What account did that fucking virus have with him? How come so many others who got the virus at the same time managed to stay alive, yet he had to die? Issa imagined there were millions just like him in every country, who felt the same—a mawkish brother-sisterhood of those who remain behind. It made nothing easier, nothing better or less painful, and with the passage of time you had to swallow your pain because folks got sick of hearing about your one measly death when people were dying in droves in one war after another across the Middle East. Solmaz had once taken him to a support group for those who had lost family to the virus. He had walked out in the middle of it. Not because it wasn't helpful, but because it was too helpful. He wanted the hurt seared into his heart, because what else did he have left to him?

That first night after teaching his class at the language institute, he had taken a walk through Daneshjoo Park with Mehran, who seemed to know everybody there. The park was a known gay refuge that Issa had avoided because of the theaters nearby and the certainty that he'd run into someone from his brother's world and not know what to do or say to them after so long.

None of this mattered now, in this theater with the flat *King Lear* production in Persian. Because it already felt like he and Nasser had entered a vortex that was inevitable and beautiful and perhaps catastrophic.

When most of the audience had left, Mehran came up and invited them to an after-party at the home of King Lear himself, a heavyset actor with limited range that Issa had already seen in several mediocre art-house films that Europeans had given prizes to because they could. Nasser wanted to go, so they went. The sprawling apartment was in one of those well-built residential complexes just north of the old American embassy before it was raided and taken over by revolutionaries. Home to mostly artists and academics, folks who held parties long into the night in the heart of the Islamic Republic and drank themselves into a stupor night after night, convincing themselves this was their way of being activists against a regime they despised but had to suffer. It was strange for Issa to find himself with Nasser in that space—Nasser appearing completely at ease and chatting with everyone, while Issa mostly sat in a corner by himself, nursed bathtub *arak* that smelled and tasted toxic, and thought about the various strands of his life in Tehran.

A text message from Jafar in Mashhad broke his reverie. The old soldier was coming to Tehran because of the possibility of spinal surgery that doctors claimed would improve his leg movement. Because of his track record during the war and the contacts he had from those days, Issa was sure Jafar would get the best treatment at one of the hospitals they reserved for the Revolutionary Guards. But the former warrior still preferred to stay in the neighborhood where he'd been a devoted karateka for so long. Issa texted him back in Arabic: *beyti beytak*—my house is your house, the Arabic banter between them stemming from their shared admiration of that oceanic language.

As the night wore on and he fell into the depths of the *arak*, his mood turned more sullen. Nasser's ease here had thrown him off guard. He hadn't expected it. By two a.m., the music was loudest. Looking across a living room filled with bodies, he saw Nasser, visibly drunk, dancing with none other than Mehran. Everybody was dancing, that regular Middle Eastern shuffle of exaggerated hips and twirling arms and wrists. He thought back to the month before Ramadan, when he and Nasser had been ready to fight for the repute of a burned woman, and now they were here, as if that other episode was something you only saw in a movie, something that could not possibly be a part of anyone's reality. A burned woman. The idea and the words got to him every fucking time, imagining himself somehow at fault for what had happened to her, at fault for a bug in the universe that would drive a woman to pour gasoline on herself and light that match. Deep down, he still wished Nasser would rip the so-called widower apart at some point, beat him beyond recognition so that he'd never bring another woman into that house again.

His phone vibrated. He thought it may be Jafar giving him a precise date for his arrival. It wasn't.

The first email contained a sentence written once in classical Arabic and then again in Persian: *Between words and silence lies a purgatory, the grave of intellect and the graveyard of objects.*

The second message was only in Persian: *Why have you stopped writing me?*

It was Maysa.

IT TOOK HIM a week to write back, and then he only sent a short note along with his telephone number and his home address.

You'll know where to find me.

His language institute class was on odd days this term. The next time he met with the students was Sunday. Mehran looked especially good that day and flaunted it. Dressed in a white jacket that looked too warm for the weather, he'd let his glistening black hair sweep over its upturned collar in striking contrast. He sat in the back smiling the whole time. As soon as class was finished, Nasser popped into the room. Issa's eyes went from Mehran to Nasser and back to Mehran. And then he resigned himself to something in the way of an explanation, although he wasn't seeking it.

Nasser looked sheepish for just a second, like he had been caught in an act, then he started to walk toward the instructor's desk, where Issa waited. Mehran did the same, but then once they were standing over Issa and he tried locking his hand into Nasser's, Nasser pushed the hand away. It was a small gesture, and it said everything.

Issa waited, watching Mehran's big smile go blank for a second. Now Mehran played the good sport, took out a little mirror from his handbag, and began rubbing cream, a little nervously, on his face.

"Well, I like my hands free anyway," he sang.

"Gentlemen, *aghayoon*," Issa began, "are we here to tell us something?"

Nasser motioned for Mehran to leave the room. Another big smile came over Mehran's face. As if he liked the idea of being told what to do without words being exchanged. This irritated Issa, but he didn't say anything.

Instead, he waited. So did Nasser. Today there was no class

afterward; they had all the time in the world for Nasser to make what Issa guessed was going to be some kind of needless confession. He neither wanted to hurry the other man along nor help him in any way.

Quietly, Nasser said, "The person who just left the room is not an *agha*. Not a gentleman. All right?"

"Well, I haven't looked down between his legs, Nasser *jaan*, but he has appeared to me very much a gentleman this whole time. And, honestly, whatever suits you. You don't need my permission for anything, if that's what you're seeking."

They were quiet for a long time. For Issa, it was as if all his history with his brother had come crashing down in the most roundabout and, frankly, absurd way.

"Nasser, what is it you want?" he continued. "Remember, I'm on your side. What are you having trouble with? You like Mehran and he likes you." He shrugged. "You are adults."

"Mehra!"

"Excuse me?"

Nasser repeated Mehran's name again without the *n* at the end of it, making it entirely another name, a woman's name. "Mehra."

"Who is Mehra?"

"The woman outside."

"But he's not a woman, Nasser *jaan*."

"Shut your mouth, Issa."

"He's not a woman. And you like him and it's fine."

"It is not fine. Not here. Not . . . anywhere." The way Nasser had said it, it was as if he was pleading.

"What do you want me to do about it?"

Nasser croaked the word. And Issa was sure his friend had

never even heard the word until just a few days ago. Actually, he wasn't sure of anything. All of this must be a dream. Who was he to judge the human heart when he didn't even know his own? He had believed he'd pegged Nasser completely; how wrong he'd been. Nasser was staring him down, and the word he meant to utter took its damn time: "Trans."

"Trans?"

"That's what they call it." He now was looking at Issa as if his friend should give him the entire history of transgender identity and guide him through it. "The Imam himself gave a fatwa about it a long time ago, I found out. It's legal in Islam, at least our Islam. A man who is not really a man can get surgery and become a woman." He paused. "Reverse too. A woman can become a man. Many people do it. The state even pays for a part of the cost. They're helping Khoda fix a natural mistake."

Issa sat there. Not quite baffled. Angry was more like it. Yes, that was what he was, angry. And he was trying to search the source of this anger, figure its contours, its shape and trajectory. Because already, he understood this craziness wasn't going to go away. He may have not seen Mehran for a long time. But he knew Mehran. Had known him for years and years. He had known the entire pageant of his brother's outcasts. That was what they'd often call themselves, *darbedar*. Laughing at themselves, crying at themselves, yet always, always knowing full well who they were and what they were and, more importantly, what they weren't. Mehran was not trans. Not by any stretch of the imagination. Not the Mehran who had hinted years ago that he wanted to kiss Issa and not the Mehran that he knew now. And to want to force him into something that he wasn't because there had been a generous fatwa or because the government paid for these things was utter bullshit. It was the ultimate intimidation, in fact. Issa wasn't going to have any of this. Not for a second.

"Nasser."

"What?"

"Are we really having this conversation?"

Nasser shrugged, "I don't see anyone else in this room. So yes, you and I are having this conversation."

"Mehran is not trans."

"Mehra."

"Is Mehran all right with you saying Mehra?"

Nasser nodded.

"And Mehran is fine with it because Mehran wants to have gender-affirmation surgery in the Islamic Republic since, according to you, nature made a mistake?"

"Gender what?"

"Affirmation."

"Well, we talked about it. Yesterday."

There was a knock on the door. They heard Mehran's voice. "Hurry, boys. We are not solving our country's problems here."

"Actually, we are," Issa muttered to himself.

It was a stalemate, and it wasn't even his business. A part of him wanted to say, "The hell with both of you. Do whatever you want. Why are you talking to me anyway? Who am I in all of this?" But he couldn't just let it go like that. It was as if the specter of Hashem was watching. He had nothing against Mehran changing to Mehra if that had been what Mehran wanted. But he suspected Mehran didn't want that. Even if Mehran came into this room right this second and pleaded for the change, Issa thought it would be coming from a place of desperation and not desire. He thought it was fantastical, grotesque of Nasser—whatever you wanted to call it. But more than anything, it was this: unfair. Unfair to force someone to convince themselves they wanted a change of this magnitude when they really didn't. It was another version of pummeling the life out of someone because you had them believing it was for their own good.

For a minute, he wondered if he'd have to fight Nasser over this. Not fight as in words exchanged. But a real fistfight, the way both of them knew how. It would be bloody, and Nasser would win in the end. But maybe only then would he be able to press home to the other man that what he was asking of Mehran was not an ask at all, but a monstrous coercion.

He regarded Nasser, not sure that what he was about to say to the other man would make a dent in him. "Look, not every man or woman attracted to the same sex is trans. Anything can happen, yes. But mostly someone like Mehran just wants to stay who they are and have you stay who you are."

Nasser looked at him menacingly. "How can you be so sure. Did you sleep with Mehra before? Are you in love with my Mehra?"

"Don't be a child."

"I'm asking."

"I've known Mehran for eighteen years."

"People change."

"They do, yes. But you are forcing something here. It's obvious."

"Answer me. Do you love Mehra?"

"It's Mehran. And yes, I love him. But not in the way you are asking. I love him the way I love you or anybody else I'd call a friend."

"You're not going to call her Mehra, are you?"

"No, with Khoda as my witness, I won't do this." He didn't feel like adding that he had spent a week with Mehran way back when, and a week with anyone was more than enough to clarify certain things about them.

Nasser grunted. "Then tell me why the state helps with the cost of the operation if it's so bad to do it?"

Now they truly were being absurd. He said, "God bless the state if they want to help a real trans person realize their dream. But that's not what Mehran wants."

"How do you know?"

Issa raised his voice. "Because I've known Mehran since he was just out of high school."

"Maybe Mehra has changed since then."

"He has not."

"You seem to know my Mehra too well."

"I know him well enough."

"But the state—"

"*Kir tu dahane* state!" Issa shouted. "Fuck them! They don't want men who like men on their hands, so they turn them into women. You think this is just?"

"Mehra is going to do it if she wants to stay with me."

"Why? You were fine with Mehran a few days ago as he was. Why the sudden change?"

"Because," Nasser looked bashful again, "I think of her as a woman. I want a woman."

"Then go find a woman."

"I want *Mehra*. She's different. She understands . . . us men."

Issa sighed. "You are killing me, my brother. Do you know what a long and intense process it is to do this? You don't just decide to have this thing done to your body and do it overnight. Have you thought it over at all?"

"I've thought about nothing else since."

"And Mehran is fine with it, you say?"

"She has no choice."

All of Nasser's fucking chivalry out the window now. Yes, Issa could have been more forceful. He could have gone out there, dragged Mehran back into the classroom, and made him confess what he really wanted. But Issa didn't do it. He was suddenly exhausted.

He uttered the least contentious thing he could and left it at that. "But I thought Mehran was taking this class so he can emigrate."

Nasser finally smiled. "Maybe we will emigrate together; maybe we won't. One step at a time, brother Issa."

Seven

The following week, Mehran did not show up at the institute two sessions in a row. When he finally did show up, he had the traces of a black eye and he did not smile once. When class ended, he was out the door quickly. Issa pretended not to have noticed, which was ridiculous. How could one not notice? He didn't want to guess what might be happening between Nasser and Mehran. He did not call on Mehran in class; besides the black eye, he wasn't really sure what name Mehran wanted to go by at this point, which he knew was absurd. Still, he was annoyed to have to think about these things. So, when another couple of Shia holidays of death and mourning came up, he decided to buy a ticket to the deep south. The saying went that in summertime by the Gulf even a dog can't be found outside during daylight. It was that kind of hot. But where he was going had served as something of a refuge ever since Hashem took him there for the first time, when Issa was finishing high school. He needed such a place now.

That night, when he visited Aziz to tell her he was going south for a while, Solmaz was there. What Aziz had dreaded was happening. Solmaz was seriously considering going back to the surgeon for the sake of the boy. It was unfair of him, he realized, but he hated Solmaz's weakness for what she was planning to do. And even when he tried to put it in some kind of context in his own mind, he still came up empty-handed. He wasn't a mother, after all. Or a father. He could not fathom human sacrifice in those ways.

He needed a good ear. But who to go to?

And, to really rub it in, to show him how sick life could be sometimes, he went to Haj Davood's office, determined to lean on the slumlord with a "let's get on with it," only to find a closed-up building and the ultimate jest: Haj Davood was dead. The whole damn neighborhood had promptly bombarded the outside of his office with those enormous kitsch flower arrangements that surely make the dead cringe. When Issa overcame his shock at this turn of events, he looked around and saw that Haj Davood's mug was plastered on every wall and shop window he could see. It was about ten p.m., and people were still out on the streets. The gym across from the real estate office was open. Bodybuilder boys hung about outside as if their mother's milk had been taken away from them. Suddenly, this outsize citizen of the neighborhood, who seemed to have been here before Tehran was Tehran, was dead. Gone. Just like that. And Issa didn't know if his troubles in this quarter were at last over or had only been transformed.

He went across the street and addressed the bodybuilders.

"How did it happen?"

One of them, chewing gum and eyeballing Issa with a bored look, said, "Who wants to know?"

"My great-grandmother."

They all knew one another and hated one another, and he wasn't in a mood to pick a fight he couldn't win but wouldn't lose so easily either. What he was saying to them was that he just wanted basic information and was willing to eat dirt for it a little bit if that suited them.

Another guy said, "Stroke." He snapped his fingers. "Poof! Didn't take five minutes, they say. Never made it to the ambulance. We always told him, 'Haji, you have to come into the gym and exercise a little. You can't just sit in that place,'" he pointed across the street, "'and eat so much sugar and fat.'"

"May his soul rest in peace," Issa said.

The men looked at him and rather than shrugging with their usual hostility, they joined in and said the same thing. They were enemies. Had always been. Bad blood didn't go away in the Middle East. It stayed. A cancer you lived with. Until you didn't. And now Haj Davood, who had given him so much grief in the past year, was six feet under and this cancer had to find another body to inhabit.

As for these guys, they were orphans now. They had to find a new *shahr-khar* to support their bloated, fictitious muscles and vanity.

The next day, Issa took the train and went south.

THERE IS A SPOT on Hormuz Island in the Gulf where the sand on the beach is bloodred, and so is the adjacent sea. It's a red that makes one believe in anything.

His last year of high school, when he was getting ready for the university exams and Hashem had brought him to this very place, they'd stood there past twilight and barely exchanged any words.

Eventually, Hashem said, "Two years ago, I heard about this place and visited. I'd come to drown myself, you know. Then I saw this water up close. It was earth talking. I know it sounds like mystical bullshit, but how can I stop living when a place like this exists? We all need a holy something or other to visit now and then, Issa. Some folks go to the mosque. Some go to the museum. I come here."

"But why drown yourself?"

"You already know why. I promised myself one day I'd do something like this. It took years to get around to it, but I had to know if I still wanted it or not."

"Did you ever think about what would happen to me, Solmaz, and Aziz if you did something so stupid?"

"Did you ever stop to consider how every day of my life was all those fucking years when we were growing up?"

"It's the thing I've considered most, Hashem *jaan*. Be fair."

"I'll be fair if you'll be fair. Of course I considered you and Aziz and Solmaz. But I had to test myself, you know. Don't you test yourself every time you have to spar with someone?"

"It's not the same."

"Everything is a test, Issa *jaan*."

"You know what I think? I think the plays you put on, that's testing yourself. I'd be afraid to death seeing a curtain lift and my actors performing something I'd made out of nothing."

"Issa, my plays don't have curtains."

"I know that . . . Why are we here, really?"

"I've been watching you taking my books off the shelves and reading them. Asking me about this and that. You want a life bigger than the dojo."

"So I do."

"Find yourself a place like here. It doesn't have to be this one. Though it could be. You'll never get a question answered on this island. But you can pretend you did. And that's all that matters."

"Did you read this in a book?"

Hashem was laughing. "Come. Follow me."

They hiked down to the water's edge. It was an impossible red. As if a shiver of sharks had been feasting here. Hashem picked up a stone. "I'm going to skip this thing over the water. If it skips three times my wish will come true. If it doesn't, I'm fucked." He threw the stone at the red sea. It barely skipped once before sinking.

"Are you fucked, my brother?"

"Of course not. That's the whole point of it. You need to find yourself a place to skip your stones. And if your stone sinks, just go ahead and do what you want to do anyway. I think Jean Genet said that."

"Really?"

Hashem laughed again. "No, not really. But I've decided to believe Saint Genet did say it. Don't forget this is the land of *One Thousand and One Nights*, Issa. Anything is possible."

Just as back then, the island was far too hot and mostly deserted. Three days in a row, Issa rented a motorcycle from a local and rode to the red beach to watch Arabia from across that strait. He didn't skip any stones. Made no wishes. He remembered when Aziz used to take them to the shrines during the religious holidays. The countless pilgrims rubbing their faces against some questionable crypt. He'd watch Solmaz and Hashem do the same because they were older and it was expected of them. The smell of rose water and pilgrims' feet and the dread of so many unfulfilled wishes in the world. Even a child could feel them. But it didn't matter. Hashem had brought him here years ago to tell him exactly this—it didn't matter. One did what one had to. And what he had to do was to take care of his people—Solmaz, Mehran, whoever. He would fight for them. The red sea told him these things.

Hashem had skipped a second stone that day. This time the thing had skimmed the surface of the red water twice. "See, brother? I'm redeemed."

"It's just two skips."

"One has to keep trying."

"How come you've never tried with our father?"

"Because he tried too hard with *me* back when we were kids. He gave it his all. You witnessed it. He is the kind of man who doesn't know the language of settling for what you can get. He thinks with a little more push and a little more purpose everything can be resolved—even me. Somehow this gay son of his might become a warrior son overnight. He doesn't know that as things stand he already has both in me."

"You're a warrior, I know."

"But for our old man, nothing in his world—no signs, no wisdom handed down through the ages—shows him that he could be mistaken. I have not forgiven his smallness, but I came to terms with it a long time ago. He, on the other hand . . ."

"He never did."

"No, never. And I brought you here today, to this body of water, because you are something between me and him. Being caught in the middle can drive a man to despair, or else it can make him wiser. Read my books, Issa, by all means. Read as much as you like. But don't ever forget where you come from; you come from Monirieh. I don't come from there; it was never in my blood. But it is in yours. Don't turn your back on it even when you've finished reading all my books. You'll get lost otherwise. I know you."

"I hate our neighborhood, Hashem."

"Don't. That's what I'm trying to tell you. I found a family for myself—all these kids in my theater, all my actors—because I didn't have another option."

He'd understood what Hashem was getting at: *Love our old man, even though I can't. One of us has to.* It seemed fair of his brother to ask that of him—and, anyway, he already did love the old man; wanting to punch the living daylights out of someone doesn't always mean you don't love them.

WHEN HE RETURNED HOME and stepped inside his apartment, Jafar was there. So was Solmaz. And Mehran.

Jafar said, "Thank you for sending me the keys to your place."

He had, knowing Jafar might be arriving for his surgery any day, mailed him an extra set. The three of them—Jafar, Solmaz, and Mehran—were looking at him in silence, as if he had intruded on them. It was obvious they had been talking for a while. There was an easy camaraderie between them that comes from a shared something.

Issa said, "Am I in trouble?"

As soon as he'd said it, Mehran burst into tears and ran into Issa's old bedroom and shut the door behind him.

Solmaz said, by way of an explanation, "Issa *jaan*, I came here to see you. I found your friend here." She pointed to Jafar, smiling.

"And Mehran? He came here to see me too?"

Jafar and Solmaz looked at him, nonplussed.

Jafar said, "He says his name is Mehra *and* Mehran."

Solmaz got up. "Tea?"

Issa nodded.

She said, "What is going on is simple. Your friend Mehran does not wish to become a woman. He has been talking to us."

"Then he has a problem."

"I'd say so," Jafar added.

Issa looked at his old friend and sparring mentor. He looked so emaciated. Years of pain could do that to you. He could walk, but the specter of pain was always there, starting from his neck and running the length of his body. The zealous pieces of shit that he had fought against had seen to that. But at the same time, there was also a youthful shine to his face in this moment.

He asked Solmaz, "So are you going back to the surgeon for sure, Madam Doctor?"

Jafar answered for her. "We have been talking about this too. No, she isn't."

"Sounds like you guys have held a regular conference here."

Solmaz spoke up, "That was why I came to see you, Issa. I've changed my mind. I cannot go back."

"Aziz convinced you not to?"

"I don't know. Maybe."

Whether it was her mother who had changed her mind or not, Issa was glad to hear it. It was one good thing wedged in between all the crappy news.

Issa said, "Are there any other problems of this world that I should know about that the two of you have been solving in my absence?"

Jafar laughed. "We think we have it all covered." He regarded Solmaz. "All those years I knew you at the dojo, I had no idea how Madam Doctor would turn out. And you didn't exactly introduce her, did you?" He laughed again.

"I wanted her all to myself," Issa half joked. "But then she goes and marries one of her professors at medical school. I wasn't good enough."

Solmaz called him a donkey good-naturedly and went into the kitchen.

He turned to Jafar, who had suddenly turned serious. "What?"

"Listen, your friend Mehran over in that room does not want to start hormone therapy and become a woman, and he does not know how to break this news to his . . . friend. Nasser is his name, yes? And Madam Doctor here does not wish to go back to her former husband. And me, well, I'm here, as you know, to have surgery on my spine. But," he smiled, "Madam Doctor says she is going to research this. Maybe I don't need it."

Solmaz called from the kitchen, "Agha Jafar, all you need to do is move around. You need to walk. Exercise. Do things. Don't listen to the people who want to force you into an expensive surgery right away. What you need is pain management."

That was good, pain management. Issa had never heard of the term. They all could use a little of that. He glanced over at the closed door of his old bedroom. Solmaz came back from the kitchen, and she and Jafar began talking quietly, as if they had known each other forever. It was strange. He excused himself and went into the bedroom.

Mehran lay on the bed, looking ghostly.

"You don't have to, you know . . . become a woman if you don't want to. And as Khoda is my witness, I cannot even believe I've lived long enough in this world to have such a conversation with anyone, Mehran *jaan*."

"You know he gets upset when people call me Mehran."

"Do you want to leave him?"

"No. I love him."

"What is it you love about him?"

"He is gentle. Mostly. Except when he isn't. No one has ever been gentle with me, Issa. I've always had to be onstage in this town. You know how that is. It's always theater. Never ends. I have to be the gay guy who entertains everyone. Because if I don't, I'm just another *kooni* to them. Nasser is my love. He's my protection. We have fun when we're alone. I make him laugh. You know what I mean?"

No, he didn't really know what Mehran meant. He was confused and annoyed and he wished he had stayed longer at the red beach on the Gulf to skip his stones and daydream of Arabia and its miraculous language.

"Live your life, Mehran *jaan*," he said unconvincingly. "Forget about what other people think or want. Be your own . . . man, I guess."

"Oh? And just forget about other people, you're telling me? Like how your brother tried to forget? You realize where that got him?"

"I do realize, Mehran *jaan*. And I don't want to talk about it."

"But it's reality," Mehran said forcefully.

"Have it your way." He sighed.

"I just want a normal life, like everyone else."

"Who has a normal life?"

"You are such a donkey, Issa."

"I know."

He ended up spending the next hour in that room with Mehran. Twice, Solmaz brought them tea and left them alone. He had not signed up for this. It wasn't his world; it was being pushed on him, and he resented it. He wanted to be that regular guy who is only the brother of the *interesting* artist. Nothing more. The guy who visits that other world now and then but always returns to the safety of his own tried-and-true routine. No, this wasn't New York City or Berlin or Paris, and he wasn't anyone's savior.

When Mehran's narrative turned to his roommate, Issa interrupted him.

"Say that again—you have a roommate? Another man? And you expect a guy like Nasser not to be upset about it?"

"He's not quite a man yet."

"What do you mean, yet?"

"But you must call him by his male name, Ramin. He used to be Rima."

"Oh. Well, that explains everything, Mehran *jaan*. Tell me, has every other citizen of the Islamic Republic decided to have a sex change now that the government helps defray the costs?"

"I don't want a sex change, you donkey. Ramin does. And the cost they cover is nothing compared to what it really costs. So Ramin has gone . . . partway." He must have noticed Issa looking at him as if he were from another planet. "Partially, you idiot. Ramin got rid of the breasts, but there's still that thing." He pointed to their respective genitals.

"Ah, the thing."

"He's a man trapped in a woman's body. And I'm a man happy in a man's body. I have no issue with myself. But Ramin does, or did. And this does not make Nasser happy. Do you understand?"

"No. I honestly can say that I am completely *kos-mokh* by this point. I am, if you'll allow me, fucked in the head. I don't understand any of this shit you are telling me."

So they began from the beginning.

Eight

The name changes turned from being a bother to something in the realm of the fantastic.

That night, he ended up having all three of them spend the night in his apartment—Mehran in his old room, Solmaz in his father's old room, and Jafar in the living room. For himself, he did something he had not done in years and slept in the dojo, using one of the worn-out karate kick pads as a pillow, like he had done so many times as a kid.

When he entered the apartment in the morning, Mehran was in the shower, Jafar was watching some news channel about point-less negotiations with some of his mortal enemies in Afghanistan, and Solmaz was back and forth between the kitchen and the bed-room. Right away, Jafar turned the TV off and Solmaz gave Issa the sort of odd look she'd give him when they were kids and word had come from middle school he'd done something really stupid in class.

"Why are you two looking at me like this?"

They both burst out laughing, which irritated him. He waited.

Solmaz said, "You have another guest. A young lady. She got here this morning. An hour ago."

Not having anything more clever to respond with, he said, "Are we certain about the gender of this one? A definite *khanum*?"

"Beyond a doubt, Issa *jaan*," Solmaz said. And with that she went into the bedroom and came back out holding the hand of a young woman Issa doubted was more than eighteen years old.

She was brown-skinned and delicate-faced, with curls that reached below her waist. Tall. Almost East African in her refined looks, a graceful, slender neck stamped with some kind of a greenish-blue tattoo-like birthmark.

"Maysa?" Issa croaked.

Jafar laughed some more.

Solmaz was kinder and only smiled. "The name you just called her is a pen name. She told us all about it. Her real name is Hayat."

He stood rooted to his spot. It felt as if Aziz had broken one of her infamous frying pans on his head. He was dazed. This young woman was probably half his age. Her name, Hayat, meant "life." He didn't know if this signified anything. What he knew was that with his own hands he had written her his address and now she was here and he had no idea what to do with her.

Hayat watched him with doe eyes. "I apologize."

For what? he wanted to ask. But before he could say anything Solmaz took Hayat back to the bedroom, announcing that the young lady had been on a bus from Ahvaz, the main city of the southern Arab province of Khuzestan, and needed some rest.

He was relieved that Solmaz was taking over. He could hear Mehran singing a plaintive old song in purposefully accented Persian from the shower. Issa looked at Jafar, still feeling staggered. Just as he was about to say something, Jafar began to crack with laughter again.

"Really, Issa? *Bache baazi?* Playing with children?"

HE FIGURED, you made yourself available, and those in the margins, people like Hayat and Mehran, came calling. Knocking on his door because there literally was no place else for them to go to.

The first thing he did was to get Hayat out of his apartment. An Arab girl from a farming family just outside of Ahvaz. Her brilliance with language was mostly self-taught. When he asked her why she had sent him on that chase to Beirut, she said, "What was I to do, Agha Issa? Out of thin air I had someone, you, writing to me, admiring my work. Was I going to invite you to our farm so you could watch my older brothers and me milk the cows?"

"There is no shame in that, Hayat *jaan.* In fact, it's probably one of the most honorable of occupations."

"And then what? After you saw us milking the cows, then what? You would go back to Tehran and I would be left exactly where I was. My father is a good man, a simple man. But he will not allow me to sign up for the university exams. Not even if I stay home and go to the university right there in our own town. A cousin wants to marry me and has proposed. A man I do not dislike, but a man who is not really my, well, equal. Do you know what it means when somebody does not occupy the places of the mind you occupy?"

Her Persian had the formal cadences of classical Arabic. As if she were not of this time. For a moment he wished he was younger, or she was just a few years older. Then he dismissed the thought.

"Yes, you would definitely grow bored with this cousin of yours after six months."

"Agha Issa, I am already bored. Even now when he and his family come to our house bearing gifts."

"What then do you plan to do, Hayat *jaan*?"

She eyed him carefully, gauging the extent of his willingness to be her protector.

"This good man, my cousin, does not deserve my boredom. He will make someone a fine husband. But I cannot be that someone."

All this conversation would take place a week later, once she was safely ensconced at Aziz's place. Solmaz insisted on it. And he was grateful to her for taking the young runaway off his hands.

There must be a reason for all this happening at once, he thought. You could not argue with chance. On a trip to the Caspian shore, he'd watched a young girl of maybe twelve resting in a field at the height of the rice harvest season, taking a break from the back-breaking work, deep into a book of poetry from Forugh—the same poet whom Jafar and Ahmad Shah Massoud had been talking about before Massoud's assassination all those years ago.

Words. They were the river that connected them all—from an Afghan guerrilla commander deep in the Hindu Kush mountains to a girl harvesting rice on the Caspian shore, and to Issa and Hayat.

He said to her, "I never imagined you so young."

"You were looking for love, Agha Issa. It was plain in your emails."

"I suppose I was. I apologize."

"No need for that. The poet says, 'The beloved are those one does not gaze upon.'"

"What, then? Should I turn blind?"

"Love is everywhere. It does not need a specific someone."

She was too young for him to tell her this was literary bullshit. And for all he knew, maybe she was right.

"How did you become so adept at this difficult language? Your knowledge of the classics is impeccable."

She smiled. "My father taught me. Beginning with the Koran. The same father who owns a farm and has us milk the cows."

"Same father who wants to marry you off."

"The very same. A good man who has made difficult choices."

"Do you realize that now you are a runaway?"

"I am almost nineteen. Not exactly a runaway. But enough of one. May God give you a long life. And now I'm under your protection."

She was.

Aziz took to her from day one, as if he had brought her a gift. This Turkish woman from the far northwest in the Caucasus and the Arab girl from the far southwest on the borders of the Levant. Meanwhile, Solmaz sent word that she was taking Jafar for a battery of tests with doctors she knew and trusted from medical school. He said he'd join them.

"You don't have to come, Issa. I can take care of him."

"You are my flesh and blood, the two of you."

He didn't bother to add that if there was a budding intimacy between them, he wanted to see its shape. He deserved this much at least.

They spent nearly an entire day at one of the best-equipped hospitals in the city. He could tell that Solmaz's rank carried a lot of weight here, and not just because at one time she had been married to the famous eye surgeon. But Jafar's name seemed to carry even more oomph in this hospital. He'd known his friend was connected to the world of high-ranked officers and men in the "system," guys in the diplomatic service and the various ministries who at one time had been his young superiors when he was a teenage fighter during the war. But this was something different. This was a reminder that there was always a payday somewhere down the line—even as Issa tried to square this knowledge with the figure of the opium-smoking invalid he'd seen recently in Mashhad.

It was at the physiotherapy department that it happened. To his mind, it was one of those Henry James moments that Hashem often spoke of. Something so subtle as to make you question if it ever happened. After a battery of exercises that had truly exhausted Jafar, the assistant left for a break. Issa stood in a corner, watching like a fly on a wall and only intervening when called on by Solmaz. Jafar was slumped in his chair, looking drained, and she put her hands under the base of his head. Today was the most movement he had had in years, Issa imagined, and not having opium probably didn't help. Jafar kept his eyes closed as Solmaz slowly massaged and stretched his neck.

Issa wasn't sure if any of this was even allowed here—sensuality on display. On the other side of the therapy area, two old soldiers were being taught to take steps using ski pole walkers. A noisy child with thick eyeglasses played with a large blue training ball on a mat in the center of the room. And in the corner near the entrance, a female doctor gave directives to a hulking rehabilitation nurse who kept smiling and nodding his head in deference.

Now Solmaz let go of Jafar's neck, took hold of one of his arms, and slowly worked her thumb from the base of his shoulder to the fingertips. She gently set the arm down and was about to switch sides when Jafar, eyes still closed, awkwardly brushed the back of her hand. It was the slightest of movements, but Issa was sure he hadn't been mistaken.

Solmaz looked at Issa, who did not look away.

She patted Jafar on the same hand that had brushed hers and walked toward Issa.

"Go now. You are not my guardian. Nor his."

Issa looked past Solmaz at Jafar. If he read anything on the old warrior's face it wasn't exhaustion; it was relief.

"You work miracles, Madam Doctor."

"You've seen what you came here to see?"

"I wasn't sure what to expect. I think my old man would be happy seeing this, though."

"This? What is it you think you saw, Issa?"

"Well, it wasn't nothing. You can't deny me that, Madam Doctor."

She smiled, then brought her lips close to his face and kissed him on the forehead. "Go, Issa. I'm a Madam Doctor, yes. And you're not. Honestly, after all these years I still don't know what you are."

He considered asking, *But what about your son?* There was something between Solmaz and Jafar. He knew that now. It was a beginning. They were still shy with each other, true. But wasn't awkwardness itself an indication? He decided he wasn't going to ask her about her son because the Madam Doctor—for all her kindness, her goodness, her contentment with shoving elixirs into the grimacing souls of the cadaver washers who wanted to look beautiful—had also accounted for something else in a man like Jafar, something significant: Jafar would be able to stand up to the eye surgeon. Jafar had the clout and the connections, despite his ruined body and his early retirement. He'd take care of her as she would take care of him. These were considerations a woman did not dismiss, especially a woman who had had her son taken away from her.

THE NEXT TIME he went to the institute to teach his class, Mehran was back. It was obvious he'd had another physical confrontation with Nasser. It was something in the way he held his jaw, and afterward, when Issa looked closely, he saw there was a slight bruise above Mehran's upper lip.

"What happened? You had another fight with Nasser?"

Mehran wasn't crying this time. There was a new determination in his face. Something that had not been there as recently as two days ago, when he'd spent the night in Issa's apartment with Solmaz and Jafar.

"I told you, Nasser's problem is my roommate. He doesn't like my roommate."

He had forgotten about Mehran's roommate. Hayat's sudden arrival into their midst had thrown off his focus.

"Tell me the name again? Rima?"

"Do not ever call my roommate Rima. Rima is a woman's name. *Ramin*. The gentleman's name is Ramin now. I told you his former name only to give you some history, is all."

"Mehran *jaan*, has all of Tehran decided to make a fool of me? Why do you all keep changing your names?"

"No one changes anything, Issa *jaan*. A person just slips into the person they should have been all along. It was a mistake."

"Whose mistake? Khoda's?"

"Khoda. Nature. Genetics. Whatever."

He tried to put himself in the shoes of someone who wishes to change the very stuff of life, the fiber they are made of. How did that work itself out? He could not wrap his mind around it. It just wasn't a place he could visit in his imagination, as much as he tried. He wasn't that freethinking yet. This much, at least, he understood about himself. At the end of the day he was still his old man's son, and he'd been raised in hard-edged Monirieh, where manhood and its meaningless tributaries had to be reestablished every fucking day of the week. Nor was this any kind of literature that he had studied. It was real life. It was hormones. It was making breasts disappear. Or adding body hair and maybe even a penis. Or cutting a penis off. None of it was a joking matter. None of it was for laughs. And when you really got down to it, the whole phenomenon was really a miracle. A blessing. Nature made right. Its errors corrected. All of that and more. But also, in the grand scheme of things, an experience as far removed from his own as one could imagine. He had some sympathy for Nasser, but also would have liked to take the other man's head off right now.

He said, "If Nasser has a problem with your roommate, why don't you just move in with him?"

As soon as he'd asked the question, he knew what the answer would be. Nasser, the tough fire captain of Zamzam, already long overdue for taking a wife, brings Mehran to live with him. What would the neighborhood say to that?

He went on, "Look, if your roommate Ramin is still a woman,

in certain body parts at least, then I don't see what Nasser's issue is. On the other hand, if Ramin is going to be a . . . how does one even say these things? If he, or she, is going to be a man-man one day, that day as you say is still a long way away." He was rambling now. "And by then, you and Nasser will have worked something out. You will either be a woman and living with Nasser. Or you will continue to be a man and living with your roommate, another guy like yourself. And, to be honest, as I'm saying all this I feel like my brain is doing somersaults on me. Mehran *jaan*, you people have me in knots and loops."

"Who is 'you people,' Issa?"

"Please don't."

"You had that coming."

Issa sighed.

They stayed quiet for a while. There was no class after his, so they could sit here in the classroom and keep going in circles.

Mehran asked, "How is the little one? Little Hayat? The one you used to think is called Maysa." He smiled.

"Don't you worry about Hayat for now. Let's worry about your situation first."

"My situation is simple, Issa *jaan*. You must go and talk to Nasser."

"Fine."

"But before you do that, you must go and talk to Ramin."

"What do I have to say to your roommate?"

Mehran looked fed up all of a sudden. "It's about loyalty."

"Come again?"

"When I came to Tehran all those years ago to work in theater, I had no one. No one at all. My father had sworn to kill me. My mother, love of my life, was too afraid to defend me. My brothers, they are still convinced I am the devil and going to hell."

"I'm sorry."

"You're not sorry, Issa. You're a regular guy who doesn't want to bash my face in or avoid me like the plague, or fuck me and then bash me in the face. That in itself is something. You deserve a medal for that. But you're not sorry for me. You couldn't give a shit about me."

"You are mistaken, Mehran *jaan*."

"Then all the more reason you must go and talk to Nasser about me. If you care, you will go talk to him."

"All right, I'll talk to him."

Mehran smiled tiredly. "You know I haven't talked to anyone in my family in years? Being Mehran is one long loneliness."

"Come now, don't turn it into a Bollywood movie."

"My point is, do you now see why it's important for me to make a go of it with Nasser?"

"Make a go of it with someone who beats you?"

"Yes."

"Mehran, loneliness, wanting protection—things like that are not good enough reasons to be with someone," Issa said without much conviction.

"Why not? Everything in life is about loneliness or wanting protection. When I was first in this huge city, who took me in and saved me from the streets? Someone called Rima. A woman who is now a man. With a transformation yet to be completed. And he calls himself Ramin."

"Ah, well, that explains everything. I have complete clarity now."

"Shut up, Issa."

Issa put his hands up in resignation.

"Ramin saved me. Can you appreciate that? I slowly found my circle of friends through him. Then I entered the theater, and I met your brother and his troupe. I survived. Ramin did all that for me. Gave me my start in this unforgiving town. Loyalty means sticking by the people who stuck by you."

"Lovely. I'm sure Ramin is a great person. And I don't care if he has a *kir* down there or not."

"Don't make fun of us, Issa. It's beneath you."

"You want to imagine everything is about someone making fun of you. It isn't. A person either has a penis or doesn't have one. There's no joke in that. I'm being serious."

"Then listen. Two years ago, when Ramin decided to change his name and become, well, Ramin . . . Are you even paying attention to me?"

"I've never focused harder in my life. Go on."

"Ramin went and told the women in his life—friends, lovers, what have you—he was going to become a man. Do you know what some of them did to him? They did what my father did to me. They spit in his face. They called Ramin a disgrace, a traitor. How could *she* want to become a man? Men were devils, they said. They stopped seeing him and never called him by his new name. I am not exaggerating, Issa. They called him a beast. Another beast like all men. Overnight, Ramin lost so many people."

"So then what?"

"Ramin becoming a man was not acceptable. Everybody, every *madar*-fucker everywhere in this world has some part of their brain made of rock, you know? The people you thought were your friends, they can turn on you in a moment. But I'm not that person, Issa.

That's what I'm trying to tell you. I'm not leaving Ramin or asking him to leave his own apartment. Unless of course Nasser asks me to move in with him as Mehran—as a man, not a woman. As myself, and not a lie. That would be different."

There was nothing to do but reach over and hug Mehran. It was the only thing he could think of at that moment. The speech was a bit melodramatic, like everything else with Mehran. But Issa understood the gist of it; it was about loyalty, friendship, the milk of human kindness.

He said, "Count on me. I'll talk to Nasser. I promise."

Mehran squeezed him tightly until Issa gently separated them a little.

"I have one more thing to ask you, Mehran *jaan*. I've been trying to understand something. But for the life of me, I cannot figure it out."

Mehran would not let go of him yet completely. The bruise on his face confused everything. Issa didn't want to make a mistake about what was the right thing to do for him.

He said, "I've known Nasser for a while now. Not for years and years but long enough. I've worked with the man. I've fought alongside him. But it's as if I never knew the guy. What makes him tick, really?"

"You mean, in a thousand years you would never have thought he'd go for me. That is your question, right?"

"The attraction between you two, I respect it. But I don't get it. It's my failure, I know. But there it is. I don't understand how he changed all of a sudden."

Mehran smiled. "Nasser changed twice in two days. First he flirted with me and then slept with me because he thought it was a challenge. He wanted to rise to the occasion. It was just another fight for him, really. But afterward the guilt came. And the shame. He could have kicked me in the butt and told me to get lost and I would have had no choice but to do as he said. It's been done to me many times. It's the story of my life, actually. But he didn't do that. Instead he asked me to change my sex. It sounds incredible, hard to believe. But here's where it gets delicate, Issa. A man who loves you does not throw you away. He tries to work through this awful wrestling match with himself and everything that he grew up with. He's not a genius, so he fails at it. But at least he tries. People like you and me, we have to give him that—if nothing else. We have to applaud him, even if he hit me a couple of times. We have to help him."

Issa sat back and stared at Mehran for a while. "How do I do that? How do I help him?"

"You will figure it out, *azizam*, darling."

Nine

Issa stood over their graves, side by side. Hashem and their old man. If in life he could never make peace between them, in death he'd force them to lie alongside each other. It was a fuck you to both for having been so unaccommodating and making his life miserable for so long. All the things that had happened in the past weeks had taught him something new, something unexpected—it hadn't all been the old man's fault. Hashem, too, was at fault; he could have tried to teach their father something besides the visceral hatred he had for Monirieh and the dojo and everything that had to do with all that brainless virility.

He lay flowers on their graves and left them there. He could never remember the names of the flowers and had long ago given up trying to learn them. But every few weeks he came here, bought nearly wilted flowers that nobody would want to steal and resell on the streets, and made Hashem and the old man share the withered bloom.

Next he went to visit Ramin, Mehran's roommate.

Looking skeptically at him at first, Ramin said, "You have to get in line if you want to beat me up."

They stood by the door of the apartment Ramin shared with Mehran in one of the back streets of the Bahar quarter. Bahar was a laid-back old neighborhood that still had a substantial Armenian population. It was all the things that Monirieh wasn't—relaxed and inclined to give ambiguity a break rather than kill it. If he ever sold the dojo and the apartment, Issa decided he'd get a place here.

"Why would I want to beat you up? Do you even know who I am?"

Ramin shrugged and stood to the side to let him into the apartment. There was a quiet tastefulness about their place that threw him off at first. He had expected something else, a place that was more modish or loud or contemporary, maybe with one of those ubiquitous posters of Che Guevara or Frida Kahlo that seemed to pop up with tiresome regularity in certain neighborhoods of the city. Instead, the place was a monument of understatement—a small living room with a simple square table and four chairs and a beige love seat next to the window overlooking the blue awning of the corner grocer. Maybe the two inhabitants of the place had decorated it as a nod to transience, knowing that their lives here existed mostly at a threshold.

On a wall by the open kitchen, however, he glimpsed a framed photograph he had not seen in years. It was a signed group photo of Hashem and his theater troupe, all of them looking slightly off-kilter, as if they had just finished one of Hashem's marathon pieces and not yet quite managed to decompress. Issa looked at his own brother staring back at him on that wall in a house he'd never been in before and thought of the wilted flowers he had just left on his grave. He would bring fresh flowers next time. It was all right if someone stole them or put them on another grave. It wasn't the worst thing that could happen.

"He was one of a kind, you know."

Issa hadn't noticed Ramin sidling up to him. They were both staring at the photo now. A young Mehran was in there too. The boy in the picture had a look of damaged innocence that he still hadn't quite lost after all these years.

"One of a kind," Issa repeated. "Sure." He pointed to Hashem in the photograph. "Take a good look at what being one of a kind gets you in this town. A cemetery."

"The cemetery is for all of us. Don't blame yourself, Agha Issa."

Issa went to the table and sat down. "Why shouldn't I blame myself?"

Ramin strolled over and sat facing him. They stared at each other. Ramin seemed to know him, or at least seemed to have known Hashem and that theater world pretty well. Which meant they must have run into each other back in the day. But in front of him now sat a smallish man with the body of a rock climber, agile and toned; try as he might, Issa simply couldn't picture him as a woman. Ramin wore round-rimmed glasses and was eyeing him with a mixture of curiosity and pity, Issa thought. He couldn't put his finger on why he should be pitied right now, but the look was there, undeniable, sitting like something moored between them.

Ramin said, "There's a world to talk about, isn't there?"

There was. But Issa went right to the heart of it: Nasser, Mehran, and this *kiri* triangle that Ramin found himself in. For everything here was about a penis, wasn't it? Having one or not having one, shedding it or adding one on. Who would have thought he would return to Tehran and have these kinds of discussions with people? At the same time, where else but here? Watch several thousand Shia men stripped to the waist standing in concentric circles, their bodies sweaty and brimming with the ecstasies of martyrdom while they flagellate themselves during ritual, and you will have seen homoeroticism at its most raw and—yes—luscious. Hashem had known something about this and tapped into it. His theater a bloodletting of religious ritual in the uneasy suit of modernism. These were not talks that Issa could ever have with his professors back in New York. Those folks fished their ideas of the homoerotic from their dismal theories and books; here people lived them. Sweated them. And died for them.

"Why not just get another apartment?" Issa asked.

Ramin smiled. "A man decides he wants to take my roommate for a partner, and I have to move out of my own place? And you, another guy, come here to do what? Be the good cop and push me a little more gently?"

"Has he threatened you?"

"What do you think?"

"He probably has."

Ramin nodded.

Issa tried to take another tack. "So us men are here to bully you into a situation you don't want to accept."

"Aren't you?"

"But aren't you now a man yourself?"

As soon as he'd said it, he realized the silliness of his logic. And Ramin immediately trapped him in it. "So now that I am a man, I can be just as much of an *avazi* as the rest of you?"

"Not all of us are fools and donkeys, you know."

"More than enough of you are."

"Then why be a man at all? Why not stick to yourself?"

"You really don't get it, do you?"

"I do. But I also want to save Mehran from having to go through an operation he doesn't want or need."

"And my leaving this apartment would fix that situation?"

"No. But it would buy me time to work on my friend Nasser and bring him around to seeing reason."

Ramin suddenly shot up, leaned his fists on the table, and brought his face closer. "Fuck your friend! I'm not leaving my own place, and Mehran is not getting an operation. Over my dead body he will." He dropped back in his chair.

Maybe in another continent all this would have been grist for some kind of laughter. But not here. People were done in for a lot less here. For nothing, really. Issa recalled again the woman who had burned herself. People doing away with themselves as an act of will in a place where will was scarce.

He gazed at Ramin and noticed grease under his fingernails. Issa liked him. He could not guess his age, but he looked young, even boyish. Issa wondered if it was the testosterone therapy that had him looking like that or something else.

Ramin said, "Why are you staring at me? I'm not a freak, you know."

"You're beautiful."

Ramin furrowed his eyes. "What did you say?"

"You're beautiful."

"Is this a joke?"

"No. I just didn't know what to expect when I came here."

"What, you expected Frankenstein?"

"I'm just trying to understand. Why give me a hard time about it?"

"Telling someone they're beautiful is not exactly trying to understand them."

"I beg to differ. It can be the first step, actually."

It went on like that for a while. A back-and-forth that neither of them had asked for but had to steer through. In the meantime, he learned a few things about Ramin: He was a part-time mechanic, and apparently a very good one. He worked at a high-end garage uptown where they specialized in foreign cars. He also ran a business venture, making sporting gear—sweatpants, tops, hats with fake foreign logos.

"Sounds like you're doing pretty well for yourself."

"What does that mean? I'm doing well for myself, so I should leave this apartment and make Mr. Nasser happy?"

"Not everything I say has a double meaning, you know."

"You sure?"

Issa wasn't sure. Maybe that was exactly what he had meant. He apologized. Probably because the entire reason for his coming here had been a mistake.

Issa said, "I don't think you should leave this place. Truly."

"And I don't intend to. This is my apartment. I own it. It's not a rental. If someone is going to leave, it's Mehran. But he shouldn't do that just because some confused guy doesn't know what he wants."

"Or maybe he does but can't deal with it."

"That too."

"Men are shit. You sure you want to become one of us?"

"Don't insult me. I'm already one."

"You mean you have the thing?" He pointed between Ramin's legs, feeling a bit foolish about it, but also truly curious.

"The thing? The thing may or may not happen. I don't need it to be a guy."

"Are you scared to take the final plunge?"

"I would be lying if I said I wasn't."

"So you are going to stay this way? In between?"

"You are insulting me again. This is not in between. It's a real place. I just don't have a dick yet. And I may even decide to never get one."

Suddenly, Issa felt wiser. It was a silly notion, but it was there. He sat looking at Ramin, thinking that the world of possibilities had brought him to this. He wanted to be in Ramin's shoes for just a day. He wanted to know.

He laughed.

"What's funny?" Ramin asked.

"Well, I can't invite you to a bar for a drink. How about to a café, then, for coffee?"

This time Ramin's smile was genuine, no bitterness in it. "How about we take a drive? I'll show you a bit of my world."

PART TWO

Ten

August came, and the burning season began. Every day there was news of another forest in flames. They seemed timed, synchronized. As if someone was putting the country on notice. Tempers flared. In Monirieh, the sporting goods stores remained empty. Fights broke out.

Issa walked the neighborhood, waiting for someone from the *shahr-khar*'s family to come and pick up where Haj Davood had left off. But no one came. Finally, one day, he saw a new sign going up in front of the man's old real estate office. Even the bodybuilding gym was shuttered after a while. He asked around and found out the heirs had been fighting among themselves. They could agree on nothing, and so bit by bit everything that the old scrooge had worked for and swindled others out of was going up for sale. It was a fitting end to a life that had been slime, and Issa didn't mind it one bit.

He wondered what would become of Haj Davood's multitude of thugs. He understood the city well enough to know that when hoodlums lost a master they could run wild for a while. But on a Friday, he came face-to-face with the guy whose ribs he'd broken. The other man gave him a wide berth and crossed over to the other side of the main street to continue walking.

At the same time he was receiving unexpected, outlandish emails from overseas. His only lasting friend from his years in America, a colossus of a Senegalese man named Babacar, wrote to say he was tired of Dakar and wanted to come to the Middle East, convert to Shia Islam, and study at the seminary in Qom where he'd heard they gave stipends to African students.

Baba, Issa wrote back, *Stay where you are, please. In fact, I wouldn't mind leaving Tehran and coming to Dakar myself.*

Babacar had been deported just two months before Issa, after getting caught in a fake marriage scheme to obtain residency papers. The sole doorman on those night shifts at the boutique hotel in Manhattan, he knew the Koran by heart, read the French classics out loud in the lobby as a way to relax during the wee hours of the morning before guests came down for checkout, and taught Issa the minutiae of Arabic grammar while Issa showed him the finer points of English and, at Baba's insistence, read him Shakespeare and the British Romantics. They had been two transients on borrowed time in that lobby near the Theater District.

"Issa, English poetry is not bad. But—how do you say it?—it holds no candle to Arabic."

"Does French?"

"Certainly not. Do not be foolish."

"Why are we here then, Baba?"

"Well, we did not come to New York to study poetry, did we?"

"Maybe we did."

"Maybe we did. Even so, Mr. Shakespeare talks too much."

"Read his sonnets instead. He talks just enough in those. He doesn't get carried away."

"It is still not Arabic poetry."

"Nor Persian."

"I wish I could read Chinese. But I am late for my prayers."

Baba would always catch up on his prayers around three a.m., occupying a corner of the lobby to do what he had to do. He was hard to miss. At that time of the night, tipsy guests would watch him with curiosity at first, and more often than not, man and woman, they'd eventually start to giggle or crack a joke. All Issa could do was keep a straight face, check them in, give them their card keys, and wish them a pleasant fucking stay in their luxury suites.

Just then, another email came in from a PhD program he'd applied to more than two years earlier, snapping him out of his recollections.

We regret to inform you . . .

Why even bother sending this now? A glitch in the universe of rejections, he supposed. And now, so many thousands of miles away, he wrote a useless "go to hell" letter to no one in particular, which he deleted after tinkering with it for the rest of the afternoon.

NASSER AND MEHRAN had been gone for over two weeks now. They'd decided the best way to work things out was to get away from the city. Go on a road trip north where no one knew them so they could talk things through. Rent a room somewhere on the Caspian shore or maybe drive right on through to the Caucasus side of the great lake to Baku in Azerbaijan or inland to Tbilisi in

Georgia. Nothing good would come of any of this, Issa already knew. You didn't talk through their kinds of problems on a trip to the goddamn Caspian shore or the Caucasus.

Solmaz and Jafar, too, were gone. To Mashhad. By now, she had taken Jafar to all the doctors he needed to see in Tehran. No surgery was necessary. What he needed was love, tender care. He had needed Solmaz. That day at physiotherapy had sealed it. Not with a bang, but a gradual understanding between two people: *We like each other, we need each other, therefore we'll work love into the equation.* It didn't have to come immediately. After a certain age, you waited to see if the ball came your way. If it did, you held on to it. Life had humbled you too much to throw that ball back into the world.

Issa said to Aziz, "Am I cursed with lovelessness, Nana? Or is it something I do that brings others together but keeps people away from me?"

Aziz was breaking her ubiquitous sugar cubes into smaller pieces with a hammer. In the yard, Ramin and Hayat were whispering into each other's ears and laughing. They were an image of not exactly love but something more, something elemental, as if anything that might have ever happened to either of them was meant to eventually bring them to this point—here in Aziz's house in the Pamenar district, whispering to each other like there was no yesterday.

It was all too idyllic.

Aziz said, "Yes, son, you are cursed with lovelessness. I have always been cursed with it." She pointed to Ramin and Hayat. "Now those two, they are busy with other things. One of them is . . . I don't know, he is someone I did not realize could exist in our world, but here he is."

"You know about it?"

"He told me himself. He comes here all the time now. He is a good sort, but I don't know what will be his kismet tomorrow. I pray for him. Sometimes I wish all men were like your friend Ramin right there. They would be less foolish maybe. I think he is the best man I ever saw."

"Nana, you mean you accept him as he is?"

"Why not? He has kindness. This is all that matters, kindness. I have known few men who were kind. I will take a man who is kind, even if he hasn't that thing between the legs." She broke a few more sugar cubes and added, "I think that Ramin should not get that thing. It is not essential."

Issa was discombobulated, not quite believing that he was having this conversation with Aziz of all people. There was something miraculous about it—there was no other way of putting it. He thought: *It's true. Why would Ramin want to get a* kir*? What difference was it going to make?*

"Nana, you talked to him about it?"

"About getting or not getting the thing between his legs?"

Issa nodded.

"He says it scares him to get it. He can't be sure they will do a good job. Then what will he do?"

"You actually have these conversations with him?"

"Didn't I say he comes here often? I said to him, 'That thing, if you get it, will only corrupt you. A man has the right not to have it.'"

Issa goaded her a bit. "How would you know, Nana? You are not a man."

"Don't be foolish. I know these things. One time I told your father he was not a man, but that he was more like a terrible king, and the injustice he brought to his son would make his life in the next world a dark one."

"You actually said that?"

"And he hit me hard on the side of the arm. But I did not budge. I did not back away. He hit me and he was ashamed of hitting me. I told him, 'Don't be ashamed that you hit a woman. In a just world, your hands and feet should be cut off for some of the things you do.'"

"What did he say?"

"He cried like a baby. He never hit me again. And I never told any of you about it. No, that thing between a man's legs is only a bother. I say, better that everyone has it taken away."

Issa laughed. "You don't mean that, Nana."

"I mean it more than you think."

She picked up her sugar cubes and went out onto the street. Soon, she would be screaming at the junkies as she offered them a dose of kindness, giving them tea and sugar and cursing the day they were born to become the inferior men they were. As she passed Hayat and Ramin, she rubbed both their heads with her free hand as if they were her kids. For a moment a wave of nostalgia and jealousy came over Issa. He resented having to call that young girl whom he'd imagined as someone utterly different by her real name now—Hayat. He was jealous of the intimacy he saw out there. He wanted a share of that and was embarrassed for wanting it.

That day when he'd first called upon Ramin, they'd gone on a long drive around the city. Ramin was so comfortable behind the wheel in that mad traffic. That had been Issa's first thought watching him drive, while going back and forth in his head feeling as if all of Tehran somehow knew the truth, and that at every traffic stop and every intersection people were onto them and gawking at them. Even then he'd envied Ramin's calm; it was as if Ramin were making up for Issa's lack of certainty by being entirely sure of who he was and what he wanted to do—but also what he refused to do. Everything in Issa's world was being turned upside down, and he had never anticipated or prepared for it.

Then at some point he began to warm to Ramin even more, finding himself with an attraction that was unspeakable and to his mind crazy. It happened when they got to the north side of town and Ramin showed him the garage he worked at now and then. Only Porsches and BMWs and Mercedes. He was called in when their mechanics came up short. Ramin had worked there long before he began hormone therapy, and some of the guys at the garage knew. At least the management did. Issa wasn't sure what he had expected when they got out of the car. It was pretty late, but the place was still open. He had hoped it wouldn't be. Maybe they would smirk at the two of them. Maybe they'd think Issa was the sidekick to a freak show. And then they were out of the car and there was nothing but respect for Ramin from the other men at the garage. Handshakes. Kisses on the sides of the cheek like all Middle Eastern men offer each other. At that moment, Issa felt an avalanche of shame. Then, looking at Ramin, he thought, *I wish I were him.*

Then he thought, *Bullshit.*

It was probably the secret that he really wanted to own. The knowledge of the absence of a *kir* between those legs. It felt to him like a mindfuck of the first order. And later, when they drove back downtown to Jomhuri Avenue, just a stone's throw away from

where Issa had snapped that man's knee under the Hafez Overpass, he had the same feeling again. Once they were inside Ramin's clothing operation, Issa saw more than a half dozen Afghan
laborers actually living there. They worked the various shifts cutting and sewing, and preferred to sleep at their workplace rather
than trek through the city to the rooms they had to share with
twenty other compatriots. None of them had papers, and there
was no better place for them to hide from the law than right here.
Ramin looked after them. Gave them real wages, which was un-
heard of. Issa saw how deferential they were. They loved Ramin in
a way almost no one loves their boss in a city like Tehran. They
would have done anything for him. You could see it in their eyes,
and none of them knew what Ramin had been, or was, and it
probably didn't matter if they did.

Toward the end of that night, he'd asked Ramin to drive them
to Aziz's place so he could check in on Hayat for a minute. Not
long after they got there, he caught a glance, a moment, a recognition between Hayat and Ramin.

"I have a job for Hayat," Ramin had said.

"I'm listening."

"She can do three days a week at the workshop on Jomhuri. She
knows how to work a sewing machine. But what I really need is
for her to keep the books and run the office. She is well educated.
I can use someone like her."

As if preordained, Hayat had become a part of Ramin's life in
the days that followed. It was curious, so easy and natural, maybe
even beautiful. Six months ago, if someone had told Issa any of
this would happen, he might have broken their arm.

Yet here they were.

There was a commotion outside. He saw Hayat and Ramin run to the courtyard door. Harsh words were being exchanged. Aziz was shouting.

Issa hurried in that direction.

The eye surgeon was out there, Solmaz's ex-husband, sporting one of those Mercedes that Ramin worked on uptown. There was another man with him, a bodyguard type, Issa could tell. Heavy-set, sure of himself, with dead eyes and maybe a flick baton in one of his side pockets. The man looked professional. It would be a tough fight, if it came to it. He'd have to tire the guy and work his legs first.

Aziz was trying to get in the surgeon's face. Ramin and Hayat each held one of her forearms and were trying to pull her back inside. The surgeon laughed. He was handsome, a bit stocky, sporting thick, lush graying hair and expensive-looking clothes. He could have modeled overpriced watches for a second-rate magazine. His face was a cold mask, and he wasn't budging from where he stood.

He noticed Issa and brushed past Aziz.

"Who are these two?" he said, pointing to Ramin and Hayat.

His words seemed to stop Aziz, and she let Hayat and Ramin pull her back to the front entrance. Some twenty paces off the junkies watched with indifferent curiosity. In another life, they might have done something. Aziz was their heroine, their mother and father, their tea and sugar cubes and summer melons.

Issa walked toward the surgeon. His goon twitched slightly, enough to show he was on point.

"Why are you here? Solmaz is not married to you anymore, hasn't been for a long time, and you have the kid. So what do you want?"

"Everything."

It wouldn't be so easy to take out the bodyguard, Issa thought. He'd fought enough to know when size mattered, and he was no Nasser. And so, this dance of a bodyguard and junkies and a famous eye surgeon and a trans man and an Arab poetess and a tough Turkish matriarch and Issa the deportee from the United States was taking place as if written on sand; it could go either way, and at that moment Issa did not know what it was that made men want and want. A fantastic hatred consumed him. All-encompassing and tribal.

"You want everything? Well, everything is not here today. And, anyway, you can't have everything. That includes Madam Doctor Solmaz."

"You don't speak for her."

"I'm her brother and that, over there," he said, pointing to Aziz, "is her mother. So yes, we do speak for her. Get lost."

The bodyguard turned for a second and told him to watch his mouth.

This was when everything could turn bad. Issa braced himself.

Then he heard Aziz swearing in Turkish again. All those exquisite curses that she decorated their childhood with, most of them reserved for Issa's old man. Rapid-fire bloodwords that Ramin and Hayat utterly failed at containing.

The surgeon raised his voice. "She had agreed to come back. She has a home. She has a son. Now she has disappeared."

Issa decided to go for it. "She's with someone else."

"You lie."

Shrugging, he repeated, "She's with someone," before walking back toward the house where Aziz, Hayat, and Ramin waited. The surgeon was shouting now, raving about the unimaginable calamities he'd inflict upon Solmaz soon.

Yes, the surgeon could do it. Or he could have—until now. Until Jafar. It wasn't some bullshit threat, but as real as those junkies who, god bless them, had begun pelting the Mercedes with stones, which served to deflect the bodyguard's attention from Issa.

Yet this small victory was nothing.

Nothing was solved, and in another five minutes, when they were all huddled inside, while Aziz was still shaking and cursing, Issa turned to Ramin and said, "I'd like an hour or two with Hayat alone."

Hayat gazed at her feet and Ramin looked at him nonplussed. "What do you mean, Issa *jaan*? I thought we understood each other."

"I just want to know what she wants to do with her life. She can't stay here forever."

"Then she can move in with me."

"Oh? You, Mehran, and Hayat—one big happy family?"

"Are you jealous?"

"I think so, yes."

"Jealous for which one of us?" Hayat asked.

"I'M SORRY I lied to you, Mr. Issa."

She said the words in soft, classic Arabic, which sounded nothing like the more throaty accent of her native southwest. The café he had taken her to was on Henri Corbin, Hashem's old street, and was bustling with the pretheater crowd. Overhearing her Arabic words, the server gave them a strange look, then gruffly dropped the menus on the table.

As the waiter turned to go, Issa grabbed the man by the wrist and said, "Next time you come to our table, be polite. Or I'll make you eat these." He pointed to the menus.

Walking away, the server muttered "Arabs" loudly enough for the nearby tables to overhear. Issa began to get up; Hayat held him down.

"Please, I'm used to this sort of thing," she said.

"You shouldn't be. No one should."

"You cannot solve the problems of the world with fighting, Mr. Issa."

She was continuing in Arabic, and he was answering her in Persian. Language gave one options; Issa just didn't know what those options were in this joint. Her Arabic created distance, a plausibility for her past actions, the territory of the other language allowing her to exonerate something in herself.

There was nothing to be exonerated for, though. They were just two people who had come to a crossroads, here in a café on Henri Corbin.

"How are you getting on at work?" he asked.

"Ramin is very good to me," she said, not meeting his eye.

"Listen, you don't have to be shy about it. He's a good man."

"He's different."

"I'd say."

"I did not mean it that way. I mean he cares that I am happy."

"You think I would not have been?"

"You were shocked when you saw me at your door that first day, Mr. Issa."

"Just call me Issa."

"I cannot."

"*Tayeb*, all right," he said, meeting her in Arabic and in resignation.

"And you were in love not with me but with the idea of me. With my words, actually. There is a difference."

"Look, I'm not here to convince you that you should be with me rather than with Ramin. I just want to make sure you know what it is you're getting yourself into."

"What am I getting myself into?"

"He's not . . ." Issa trailed off.

"Normal?"

Issa shrugged. "I mean, what if your family were to find out?"

"Ramin is going to go down there and propose to them."

Issa sat there in stunned silence.

She said, "Why do you look at me like that, Mr. Issa?"

"Everybody and their mother is getting married," he mumbled.

"Mehran and that man, Mr. Nasser, are not getting married, I do not think," she volunteered. "But perhaps Madam Doctor Solmaz and Mr. Jafar might."

Their server came back looking sheepish, accompanied by a woman who introduced herself as the manager. She began with an apology and segued into an unnecessary explanation. They listened. The fellow's father had apparently been "martyred" by the Iraqis during the war. She apologized again, telling them that martyr or not, that kind of behavior from an employee was inexcusable. She'd noticed the exchange from afar and the tab would be on the house. She smiled.

Issa ordered two coffees and a lemon cake and stuck his hand out to the server. What else was one to do? The long memories in these lands were poisons you could not just brush under the table.

"My uncle, too, and my oldest brother," Hayat suddenly said.

They all turned to her.

"Whom should I hate, sir, for the deaths in my family?" she asked. "It was war. My brother and my uncle, both of whom I never got to see, and your father all died fighting on the same side, for the same country."

Issa, the server, and the manager all looked at her, a bit dumbfounded.

She offered some words of classical poetry: "*Your perception of the near is distance, as your perception of the far is distance, I am that faraway near devoid of distance.*"

Issa tried to keep a straight face, while the manager and the server retreated like they'd just stuck their fingers into an electrical socket. Hayat had quoted from an Arabic sequence she had translated into Persian. Issa hadn't a clue what she exactly meant by it, but somehow it seemed appropriate.

"You can possess me, Mr. Issa, if that will make you feel better," she said suddenly.

"What did you say?"

"You are angry with me and with Ramin. We will, *inshallah*, get married. But you can possess me before that, if you wish. I do not mind."

"Is this your idea or Ramin's?"

"Mine."

"Do I look that pathetic?"

"Men are a problem."

"I don't need to possess you, Hayat *jaan*."

"I will talk with Ramin then. Maybe it is he you wish to possess."

"Nobody is possessing anyone. Stop this talk."

"When you look at me or at Ramin, there is a disquiet. This disquiet comes not from a love of me. Perhaps it is from a love of Ramin. I can read minds."

He sighed. "Can you stop talking like the Koran?"

"The Koran does not sound like this. And I cannot talk any other way. My family says I am a book. Maybe I am a book. But I am not the Koran."

"I'm sorry about your brother and uncle dying in the war. I didn't know."

"Many died back then. It was before my time. Where I come from, it is full of death. But it does not change the fact that I think you should possess one of us—myself or Ramin."

"What I want is for you to stop this nonsense talk. Now tell me, how do you think your father, your family, and that cousin of yours who wishes to marry you will react when they find out you have a suitor whom you met after running away from home?"

"I do not know. It is possible they will want to kill me to save their honor."

"Well, are there any other options besides that?"

She thought about it. "Ramin will convince them. I have faith in him."

"Having faith in these circumstances is not enough, young lady. When Ramin goes to propose, no one must know his secret. You understand this, right?"

"I am young but not a fool, Mr. Issa."

Eleven

The man whose wife had burned herself looked happy. Issa watched him for three afternoons in a row from across the street at a construction site in Zamzam. At sundown, the Afghan laborers who worked and slept at the site gathered about and had two of their youngest boys dance for them. It was a lascivious dance, filled with innuendo and possibility. From the half-finished edifice that he found himself in, Issa could see right into the man's home on the other side of the road when the curtains were drawn open, the very home inside which his wife had torched herself. The fire, while enough to kill her, had obviously not been enough to cause much destruction to the house. The widower had fixed the damage in no time. From his comings and goings, it appeared he was in some kind of construction business. The double-paned windows still had the stickers on their paneling, and a brand-new metal garage door with little red balloon shapes welded on was now being installed.

Coming here was a waste of time. Issa already knew this. He'd do absolutely nothing about this man. Unlike Nasser, he wasn't about to take anyone's revenge for them. How naïve he'd been. No wonder that Hezbollah security detail in Lebanon had laughed at him; there always seemed to be a new punch line to being a donkey.

There is not only need for tenderness, there is also need to be tender for the other.

He recalled how a professor in New York would quote from Barthes's *A Lover's Discourse* in his graduate class, and then joke about how, in his younger days, he'd used the text as an entry point to his liaisons. And the graduate students of course laughed dutifully at the man's witticisms around the seminar table. Issa's mind traveled from that rarefied world to these Afghan laborers who, having escaped from the nightmares of their country, were also in need of an ugly tenderness. And so the twelve-year-old boys danced downstairs before being tossed around half-built rooms at the end of an evening.

Had the woman who had burned herself known a sliver of tenderness? Issa was still trying to understand her. Gasoline? Some other fluid that might ignite even faster? Did you pour it on and simply light a match? How long does it take before you begin to smell your own burned flesh and how long before you expire? These were easy things to discover. Just do a search on the internet. Women were burning themselves in the provinces all the time, so he'd heard. But here, in Zamzam, in the middle of the capital? Why?

When he first asked to keep lookout in the building, the Afghan foreman had asked him, "Why do you want to spend your afternoons up here?"

"I have unfinished business."

"You are lucky you were not born in Afghanistan or your whole life would be unfinished business."

Issa offered more money than the man would make in a month as foreman.

"I won't bother you but for a few days."

"You are not a bother, *agha*. Where I come from, everybody is always taking revenge on everybody, and everybody is always dying. Don't do anything to get me in trouble here. I don't want to be sent back to Afghanistan."

Issa promised.

Now here he was, on the third day. And the man whose wife burned herself and his comrades were laughing as they stepped out of a white car. Five of them. How could this man be so jubilant? Where was his wife buried? Was there even enough of her left for a burial?

Every now and then, the Afghan foreman would pop his head into the room to check on Issa, no doubt afraid that he was either crazy or planned to do something crazy.

Issa imagined that he could now understand what Nasser went through every day as a fireman. Sniffing that burned flesh from the destroyed Plasco building, and probably from other buildings, too, where nothing remained to save but the debris of bones, half-burned toys, and half-lived lives. Nasser, he decided, was a softy, despite all that testosterone. He'd confided to Issa how before becoming a fireman he had ferried illegal Afghans from the other side of the border all the way to Tehran. "Issa, you won't believe how many bodies, men and women, you can pack in the trunk of a car." After his third run, when he'd opened the trunk and two of those bodies were suffocated and dead, he'd given up on the job. When you were in your twenties and didn't have any other prospects, you didn't quit a lucrative job like that, Issa thought, not even with dead bodies in the trunk.

At twilight on his last day in Zamzam, Issa descended from the room and saw the laborers at it again. A boy was gyrating in a way that turned the faces of those men grotesque. He told the foreman that he would not be returning and thanked him. "But do you think it's right to have boys their age dance for your men like that? What happens afterward? What happens tonight?"

"Be on your way. And Khoda bless you. Don't judge us when you don't know what we go through to stay above ground."

"Why not judge you? It's wrong, what you do."

"Nothing is wrong. Do I ask you why you've been coming here every day this week? Everybody has business to attend to, *agha jaan*. Do you want to go and ask that boy if he's unhappy to be here? If he were back in his village in Afghanistan, he'd be under the village. He wouldn't be alive. Probably none of us would. It's that kind of a country."

"That does not excuse anything."

"It excuses everything. But you will never see it my way."

"No, I won't."

"Be on your way then."

HE SPENT THE REST of that week at the theater. First a *Hamlet*. A tired affair where they all dressed in modern clothes and talked in slang. *Hamlet* in implausible and poorly executed street Persian. Next a play about refugees. Except the actors looked like they'd been drinking aperitifs all afternoon. On the third night, he saw a play in which the mother of the family eats her children.

A political play. It would probably get shut down, its symbolism too obvious—the revolution, the state eating its own citizens.

He had forgotten just how bad almost all theater was.

On that third night, he noticed Nasser's car across the street. Nasser was sitting there looking directly at him. As he started to cross the street, a hand tapped his shoulder.

"Issa, are you spying on us?"

It was Mastaneh, or Masti, one of his brother's old drag queens. She carried a huge red handbag and the black wig she wore was just slightly covered by a mustard-colored shawl doubling as *hijab*. Back in the day, Masti would adapt Mexican soap operas for her own skits in Hashem's plays. She had even learned just enough Spanish to take her act on the road and was paid handsomely for doing her numbers at underground parties across Tehran.

"It's good to see you too, dear."

"I know that man in that car. He is with our own dear Mehran, isn't he? I've seen them around together. He is your friend, I think."

"Yes, he's my friend."

"Well, let's go then. He has a car and I have a party to go to. I'm taking you with me. You can't say no."

She left Issa no choice. As they approached Nasser's car together, Nasser seemed to tighten up. Masti quickly climbed into the back seat, but Issa hesitated and the two men regarded each other through Nasser's side window.

"How did you know I was here?" Issa asked.

"I find people."

"You could have just called. I'm not hiding from you. Where's Mehran?" As soon as he asked the question he knew. Something had happened. Again. He glanced back at Masti.

She winked. "You fellows have an issue. I can tell. I will wait till it is resolved."

Issa turned to Nasser. "Do I need to call Mehran?"

"I want you to hear me first."

He didn't really want to call Mehran and he didn't want to hear whatever it was Nasser had to say. Not now, anyway. He said to Masti, "Come, dear, we'll take a cab to your party."

From the driver's seat, Nasser reached for Issa's wrist and grabbed it. "I'll give you and your friend a ride."

Issa rotated his wrist and put a reverse lock on Nasser's and then pressed the other man's fist against the edge of the open window. He could tell Nasser was hurting but wasn't going to show it.

"Issa, if I get out of this car, I will deliver you a lot of pain."

He let go of Nasser's wrist. Masti was now standing next to him, her jaw open in shock.

"You guys really do have a problem," she said.

"Shut up, slut," Nasser growled. "You two are going somewhere. I know. Where? Wherever you are going, is Mehra there?"

Masti put a hand to her own face as if she'd been slapped. "I'll call the police. What is this man saying, Issa? Is he crazy?"

Keeping his eyes on Nasser, Issa said, "Not crazy. He just doesn't know who he is. There's a difference."

The moment passed. Nasser didn't get out of the car. Issa took Masti's hand in his own and they walked away.

IT WAS ANOTHER after-theater party, like dozens that Hashem had taken him to back before the sickness made these gatherings impossible for him. Familiar faces from as far back as two

decades ago, older now, ones that would boisterously cut one another down at the dinner table. It was an extension of the theater
in a way—theater, and excessive familiarity. As Issa turned to
Masti to tell her he would leave right after dinner, she put a finger
to his lip.

"Do I dare ask you what that was all about with that man?"

"Like I said, the man doesn't know who he is."

"Issa, I didn't know who I was until I was almost thirty. So
what if he doesn't know?"

"So nothing. He just shouldn't hurt other people for it."

"Hurt as in injure?"

"Yes, that kind of hurt."

"You mean to tell me he is hurting our poor little Mehran?
What do you plan to do about this?"

"Mehran isn't my charge, is he?"

"He certainly is. Our world here is small. Everybody knows you
introduced this man to Mehran."

Issa drew in his breath. "Please don't tell people about this," he
said. "I really mean it."

"About what? That you introduced them, or the fact that Mehran is being beaten?"

Half a dozen conversations were going on at once across the loud
dinner table. Masti's eyes had that glow. It wasn't one of amusement or sarcasm or empathy. It was a fuck you. *Fuck you and your
condescending ways. You stoop into our world for a minute and you think
you can tell us how to be?*

"Forget it. I'm sorry."

"You're not sorry, Issa. You are not sorry at all. You judge us,
you judge *me*, too harshly."

"I'm not judging anyone."

"Do you know what it means to live in a police state?"

"I think I have an idea."

Issa passed the tray of rice that was circulating around the table and someone else drank a toast to Hashem's memory as guests hit their spoons against their bowls and cups. Some others who'd gotten up from the table earlier were already dancing.

"You really don't have a clue, do you, Issa? There are a few thousand of us who run into one another all the time, week after week, in one miserable dinner like this after another. Because there's nowhere to go, nothing else to do."

It wasn't true, of course. There was always too much happening in a city twice the size of New York. But he wasn't going to argue over it with Masti.

She went on. "Come to the theater again tomorrow and I'll take you to another dinner and it will be exactly the same people doing and saying exactly the same things. We're like a crowd stuck in purgatory at a bus station. Condemned to one another's faces till the end of time."

Issa was looking at the old queen and recalled an act in which she would sing the classical verses of Omar Khayyam, accompanied by a drum, with bright red plumes streaming from her wig. It was a twist on a traditional act from down in the Gulf, one that brimmed with pure joy, even if the poems were mostly about the impermanence and briefness of life. People turned into sad sacks for all kinds of reasons; living in a police state was just an excuse. In a moment of clarity, coming from drinking just the right amount of *arak*, Issa realized that Masti had become angelic with age. Tender and melancholic. It was beautiful to watch.

"Aren't you ever afraid," he asked, "that they'll break the door down at one of these gatherings and haul you all in?"

"For being us?"

"Yes, for being you."

"There is always that chance. I've been hauled in before and had to pay a good amount of money to get out. But," she gestured around the room, "see the dense cigarette smoke here? There's always a snitch among us and they are just like this smoke. The smoke sits or changes shape, but it's always there. The snitch gets himself into some kind of trouble, and now he has to report on his own friends. But what's there to report? That Masti doesn't eat meat anymore? Handsome, we are on no one's list of people to watch. And even if we were, then we are far at the bottom of that list. We are nothing. We are zero. We don't even care about politics."

The music got louder. A young woman came at them smiling and tried to get Issa to dance with her. Issa said a polite no. Then Masti good-naturedly slapped the woman's hand away. "He's with me," she said. Turning back to Issa, she added, "At least we, your brother's people, don't seem to put you off anymore. That's a good thing."

"You are being unfair. I never felt that way."

"Oh come, you know what I mean. We were always just a curiosity."

"What's wrong with being a curiosity?"

"As you wish." Masti surveyed the room pulsing with bodies, then turned away.

Issa noticed tears were now streaming down her face, smudging the mascara. "What's wrong?"

"I saw Mehran, you know. Saw him with that tough-looking friend of yours. Is it love? Is that why he's beating the poor boy?"

"Maybe it's that. I don't know anymore."

"And you? Have you loved, Issa?"

"Love avoids me. It's like I have the plague or something."

"Really? You too? I tried to be good to a boy half my age once. He'd come from the provinces. A junkie. Oh, what a mistake I made, Issa *jaan*. Do you know what the last thing he ever said to me was? 'I either take all your jewelry, or I beat you up and then take your jewelry. Which will it be?' That was about as close as I ever came to love in this angry town, if you can believe it. I let him take the jewels. But he decided to beat me anyway. Not too many people know about this. I don't even know why I told it to you. Maybe because you are the brother of my dear old dead friend. Maybe because your manly friend is hurting Mehran. If you ask me, forget love. It's not for people like us. We're not lucky that way. Love is mostly about waiting. And we have no one to wait for."

He planted a kiss on Masti's forehead. "I must go."

"I hope you are going to look after your friend, and my friend Mehran."

"I don't know yet, to be honest."

Masti reached for his hand and held it. "Issa, walking away is dying. You do understand, don't you?"

He nodded, planting another kiss on Masti and squeezing her hand. He saw himself out, carefully tiptoeing past the dancers. People were still smiling at him, inviting him to stay. Hashem's brother. Their dead hero's brother. Such invitations were only Persian courtesy at ten p.m., the beginning of the night, before folks drank too much *arak* and burned the evening down to nothing. And there was nothing wrong with that.

MEHRAN WAS WAITING for him in front of the dojo.

Issa could barely stand to look. There was no way to hide the black eye this time.

A half hour later, he was outside Nasser's door in Zamzam. As soon as Nasser opened it, Issa delivered a straight lunge punch to his face. Nasser fell backward into his living room, collected himself, and for a moment it seemed like he was going to attack Issa. But he didn't.

"It was why I came to you," Nasser said, holding his jaw. "I don't know how to do this, brother."

Issa walked inside Nasser's apartment and shut the door behind him. "It doesn't mean you have to put your hands on him."

"I don't know anything else."

Neither of them did, Issa realized. Their inheritance was violence. It was all they knew. Even Hashem's library that Issa had devoured, and all the books he'd read afterward, none of it had prepared him for tonight. It would always be this: violence lurking in the shadows. Men like him and Nasser, as different as they were, ultimately were only fluent in that one language, and their loneliness could not be countered with a love affair, or any love at all.

"Hit Mehran one more time, and you'll have to fight me."

"I want to know what has happened to me."

Saying this, Nasser fished a bottle of *arak* from the freezer and sat himself on the other side of the counter in the open kitchen.

Issa joined him.

"I want to know what happened to you too."

Nasser offered him a shot glass. "You mean you want to know how I turned into a *kooni*?"

"Don't use that word."

"What am I then if I'm not a faggot?"

It felt stupid, but with Nasser they were always one step away from the classroom. "Don't say that word. Nobody uses it if they can help it."

"You think I didn't know that? What the fuck does it even matter?"

"It's about how you see yourself."

"Is this one of those therapy sessions you talked about before?"

"If you want it to be."

"What are *you*, Issa?"

"With the Messiah as my witness, I wish I were a tiny fish in the ocean and lived for just a day, or that at least I was born somewhere civilized and boring. Denmark maybe. Or Switzerland."

They mulled this for a while, and then Nasser said, "I like hitting Mehran."

"Then you are one sick bastard. What do you mean, you like hitting him?"

"I don't mean it like that. I like to wrestle with him. I actually teach him moves. You know, wrestling moves. Then other times we get to talking about the operation he should have and that's when he makes me angry. It's that roommate of his. That man-woman who keeps telling him not to have this operation on my account. I'm going to deal with that Ramin fellow."

"You touch Ramin, and again you'll have to fight me."

"So I'll fight you. And beat you."

Issa's shot glass was still full. He threw the content in Nasser's face. "Do it now, you whore's son, if you're man enough."

Neither man moved. Issa could see the veins in Nasser's temples twitching. It was the kind of anger that was still trying to find its focus. Issa waited. Nothing.

He said, "Nasser, there is absolutely nothing wrong in liking another man."

Nasser's fist came down hard on the table. His own shot glass flew off but didn't break. The bottle fell sideways, and Issa picked it up.

"Am I going to take Mehra to my mother and father and tell them, he's the one? I'll lose my job, my life, everything. They'll run me out of Zamzam."

"No one will run you out of anywhere."

"Oh? So your brother—he had an easy time of it?"

"It's not the same thing, Nasser *jaan*."

"The Messiah as my witness, it's exactly the same thing."

Issa got up and walked about. There were all kind of plaques on the walls of the living room honoring Nasser for his courage and leadership as a fire captain. Photos of him in various firehouse competitions in which he and his team had always come first. Photos of him in the army. Always in the center of things. The natural leader. The guy everyone else looked up to. You could tell all this from his easy gaze at the camera and the way everyone else sort of fixed their eyes and their smiles according to his.

Issa called from the living room, "Did you always know this? I mean . . . about yourself?"

Nasser poured both himself and Issa another drink, avoiding eye contact. It was another half hour before he answered.

"No. I didn't always know."

"Are you lying?"

"I don't know. It wasn't in the accounts, you know what I mean? Being a *kooni* wasn't in my book of life. It was there in the world. I saw it. I made fun of it. But it wasn't in my house, in my yard, in my room, in my mind."

"What changed? I mean, what changed that day when we went to the theater together?" Issa watched the other man, who was still nailed to his chair in the kitchen. They were at the threshold of something. He wasn't sure what. He went on, "Remember what you said some time back? You said, 'Every time a woman burns herself, the world ends.'"

"Yes. So?"

"When you hit Mehran like that, it's the same thing."

"What changed, you want to know?" Nasser was now slurring his words, the empty bottle sitting between them. "That theater. The way your friend looked. All those people. That party. I'd never known any of this. I decided to just go along with it."

"And you still can."

Minutes passed. No answer.

Nasser's head was on the table, his hand wrapped around an empty shot glass. He had already begun snoring.

Twelve

The Afghan foreman said, "You came back sooner than I thought you might."

"How did you know I'd come back at all?"

"You said you had unfinished business, and I know something about men who live with unfinished things."

They sat in darkness in the same room Issa had occupied earlier in the week. The foreman had rolled himself a thick, cigar-sized smoke made of tobacco and *chars* and offered it to Issa. It was impossibly strong Afghan hashish, and the first hit threw him into a coughing fit, which made the foreman laugh. From somewhere in the building, they could hear moans of dispassionate sex, brutal in its cold concentration on orgasm. Men going at it with unwavering focus after a hard day's labor in an unfriendly country that blamed them for every theft and murder that took place here. The sounds were like knives in Issa's brain, and he took a second hit of the *chars* to drown himself.

The foreman pointed across the street to where the man whose wife had burned herself lived. "Your unfinished account lives there."

"That he does."

"What do you plan for him?"

"I haven't decided yet."

"What did he do?"

"His wife burned herself."

"He burned her, or she burned herself?"

"You could say that it was both. He drove her to burn herself."

"And you are?"

"A concerned citizen," Issa said, a fog of *chars* hooding his eyes.

This made the foreman start laughing again. Somebody in one of the lower floors of their half-done building was finally having his damn orgasm. The sound was elemental and wild. It crept up into the eddy of one's high and ruined it.

Issa kept his eyes on the house across the street. One of only two houses on that block, the rest were new, hastily built apartment buildings. Real estate was booming in this discount neighborhood. Soon, the man whose wife burned herself would build another faceless five stories over his land and make a killing from it.

And what was any of this to him? He was knocked flat by the *chars*. As was the foreman. The drug's haze drifted between them like a shared pet. The moment was theirs, two strangers with a half dozen wars and ten thousand couplets of classical Persian verse across their mutual border.

Issa began a drug-induced sermon on love. He spoke of going to Beirut and feeling like a fool doing it.

The foreman answered the call. "I never stop believing I am

loved. I refuse to get to that place, *yaar*, where I must ask why I am not loved."

"Who said this? Mawlana Jalaluddin of Balkh?"

"No, friend. That is me, your humble servant speaking the truth. Because we must die for we have known them, die of the inevitable flower of their skin, die of women."

Eyes closed, Issa asked, "You said this also?"

"No, *yaar*. That was a certain Mr. Rilke. A German poet."

"I know who Rilke is, brother. But how do you, of all people, know Rilke?"

"An Afghan cannot know Mr. Rilke?"

"I am just curious."

"I was in the war. But first this: in my country you cannot say, 'I *was* in the war.' Because everybody is in the war all the time. So this sentence makes no sense in Afghanistan because it is in the past tense. You can only say it outside of Afghanistan. So . . . I was in the war. One day an American convoy ran over my only son. It was not done on purpose. I did not blame them. No, I take it back; I blamed them. But not in the way you blame someone for deliberately killing your only son. I blamed them because their actions made the accident possible. It did not have to be that way. You see?"

"Yes, I see."

"Someone gets out of the convoy, comes up to me, and hands me a one-hundred-dollar American bill in compensation for my sorrow. My son is freshly dead and this man in a uniform gives me money for it. How much? One hundred dollars. Then the soldier gets back in his vehicle and they drive off. I still have the bill."

"Just like that?"

"With Khoda as my witness, just like that."

Issa gave his full attention to the foreman now. He felt sweet inside, and cooked. He was watching himself watch this Afghan stranger who quoted Rilke while they both staked out the house of the man whose wife had burned herself. There was a light on over there. And there was movement on the first floor. Issa could not tell if it was the widower or not. Someone coming and going into a room that may have been the kitchen.

The foreman blew smoke. "Inside my country you cannot say, 'Everyone I had is dead.' Because everyone loses everybody over there. I was not special. I only had my boy left in that country. And after they threw that hundred-dollar bill at me, I went and joined men fighting the Americans. For a while. I killed, but my heart was not in it. So I escaped and went to India. I loved India and stayed there awhile. But India did not love me back. I wanted to go to Australia or Japan, anywhere far, far, far from where I came from. Or die trying." He pointed to the house across the street. "Look, your man is coming out."

It was true. The widower was getting in his white car. Issa watched him as if from miles away. He had almost forgotten why he was there.

The foreman asked, "What did this man really do?"

"He burned his wife, I already told you."

"You said he drove his wife to burn herself."

"He did."

"Then he should pay for it."

"Well, something should happen to him. But forget him for a minute. Obviously you never got to Japan or Australia, did you?"

"I went the wrong direction and ended up on a Greek island.

Two years there. It's where I learned Mr. Rilke. A good German taught me that. He was there to help us. One of those good people who come to help because they are good. You know? He taught me many poems, but I like this one best. Because it is very true. We must die for women."

"Well, that whore's son who just drove off, his wife died for *him*. It was the other way around."

"Then we have to reset the balance of the world."

"What did you do before they killed your son and you became a refugee in Greece? And how did you end up here in Tehran?"

"I was a schoolteacher. Let me tell you, I know chemistry. I know physics. But that was another lifetime ago. After two years, and despite the help of this good man from Germany, they sent me back to Afghanistan. No, the truth is I asked to be sent back. I could not stand being on that island anymore. Then just one day back in Afghanistan, I knew I had to leave again. The ghost of my son was everywhere. And the ghost of everybody else. All the ghosts all the time. Now I'm here. I'll stay in your country if you'll have me."

"My house is your house."

He didn't know how long he fell asleep there. When he woke up, dawn was coming and the foreman was doing his prayers. Tea brewed on a thin little gas stove. Issa poured himself some. He could hear the sounds and movements of the other laborers.

He left a wad of cash where he'd slept, patted the foreman on the shoulder as the man was finishing his prayer, and started to leave.

"What will you do?" the foreman called to him. "I mean, about this imbalance in the world. Or the imbalance on this street, at least. Know that you are my guest here anytime you want."

Issa nodded his thanks. The sound of the muezzin was trailing off somewhere, and as he was leaving the building, he saw one of the two boys who danced for the older men standing in a corner praying quietly by himself.

Thirteen

Back in his own apartment, he saw that Nasser had shown up, probably guessing he'd find Mehran there. He'd guessed right. Now the two of them were sleeping in something of an embrace—Mehran lying on the sofa, his battered face turned away from Nasser, who sat with legs splayed on the floor, the right side of his own face pressed into the back of Mehran's right thigh in what must have been a gesture of remorse. It was a picture of misfortune, or rather of more misfortune to come, and it made him want to awaken them both and throw them out of his place. The fog of the *chars* he had smoked with the foreman was still strong, though the sweet sensation was now gone and replaced with something far less pleasant. He wished it were Ramadan again and he could take refuge in the shell of piety and hunger that the month afforded.

But next Ramadan was far away, and in the big bedroom where his old man and Hashem had once shared reluctant space, there were two more people sleeping—Aziz, perfectly straight on her back, hands pressed into her chest, mummy-like, and Hayat, rolled into a ball, a palm resting on Aziz's shoulder.

Aziz had not been to the apartment in years. Something must have happened. Issa considered the situation: until just a few months ago, his life had been one of the unrelenting loneliness of a returned immigrant. Now he was practically running a motel. Strange how everything could be upended in a matter of weeks.

He sat in the smaller bedroom and turned on the computer. There were so many cases of self-immolation by women that he didn't know where to start. Especially in the southwest of the country, where it had turned into something of a fashion for young women to kill themselves. He read the statistics, pored over reports in one online paper after another—poverty, girls married off far too young, narratives of domestic abuse that defied imagination. Attempts with the rope, with pills, jumping off cliffs or drowning or self-stabbing. But none seemed to have as much of a success rate as burning yourself. A girl that a paper had interviewed in the hospital spoke of perfect happiness now that she could not feel any pain; apparently once you felt no pain from the burn damage, it meant your nervous system was shot to hell and it was only a matter of days or hours before you died. Two days later, the girl was gone.

Issa passed an hour like this, maybe two. Women beaten not just by their husbands, but the entire family—usually by the husbands' mothers and their own brothers—because they had dared attempt suicide. Brought down from the noose just in time only to be beaten again and again because the family didn't want the disgrace of a suicide on their hands. Beaten because it was raining or not raining that day, or because they had given birth too soon or too late. Beaten because being beaten was there to be administered. Like a refrain, a chorus, a seasonal song. Beaten because some *madar*-fucker had woken up on the wrong side of the bed that morning, or because the piece of shit didn't have a bed, or because he didn't like his bed, or because of what or whom was on his bed. It was that simple, that easily accomplished. He followed the maps of the places where these things happened, read more statistics, read interviews with the handful of psychologists who ventured into such end-of-the-world places where a woman burned herself every seventeen days. Yes, there was a place like that, among the Lors of a certain district, the very tribe of his father and grandfather and great-grandfather. Every seventeen days. He zeroed in on that number, trying to cull some meaning out of it, but none would issue. It was what it was. Seventeen days.

"What are you reading, Mr. Issa?"

Hayat was standing over him, peering at the screen. He felt embarrassed. "I'm researching something."

"A girl in my school did that to herself once. She didn't die. But . . ." She didn't finish the sentence.

Issa felt naked sitting there like that. As if he had been caught watching pornography. To get off that web page, he opened his email. There was a message from Babacar in Senegal. Two words: *I come.*

Hayat was still watching him. He sighed and wrote, *Jesus Christ, Baba. You can't just get up and come here to become a Shia cleric. Who put this craziness in your head over there in Africa? But if you can afford the ticket and a visa, what the hell. Come, my brother.*

In truth, he loved the idea of Baba here. It was just this foolishness of wanting to become a cleric that annoyed him—and mostly because it wasn't all that difficult to do it. It was strange: their uncertain lives in America transferred back this far to the east. All those evenings of Babacar showing up each night at the hotel with his stacks of textbooks. The English vocabulary and grammar. The man wanted to speak perfect English the way he did French. And when Issa asked him about the speed with which he was able to pick up English, Babacar always went back to the Koran. *I learned the Holy Book by heart since young-young. If you memorize the Book, you can learn everything fast-fast.*

"You are writing to a friend?"

He looked up at Hayat. "Huh?"

"You are writing to a friend, yes?"

"I am indeed. And you know what? You remind me of him."

Hayat stayed silent.

"You and him, Hayat *jaan*, you don't just talk like books, you are books. He has an idea to come here to become an *akhund*. He is from Africa. West Africa. Can you believe this Muslim West African man wants to come here and study Shia law?"

"Why should I not believe it? Men do many things, all things, good and bad, and they have their reasons for doing them. Do you think, Agha Issa, that what your friend wants to do is such a bad thing?"

"I don't think it's a bad thing at all. He is more than welcome to come here. I just don't understand his reasoning, you know?"

"For wanting to come here?"

"For wanting to switch gears."

"Gears?"

"The man is a Sunni Muslim already."

"He wants a change."

"What difference does change make, Hayat *jaan*? Sunni, Shia, it's all—"

"Not the same. One theater is different than another theater."

"There you go again, speaking in riddles."

"I make you uncomfortable."

"Well, Hayat *jaan*, you certainly don't make me comfortable, if you want to know the truth."

She pointed to the computer. "Why read about burned women, Agha Issa?"

"Because there are a lot of them in this country. You just told me about one case yourself."

They went silent again, and Issa could hear the others stirring and moving about the apartment.

"Ramin went south, you know. He went to propose to marry me."

"Just like that? He was at least supposed to let me know before going. Have you all gone mad?"

"I asked him to wait for you. But he would not wait. Now I am afraid my family will hurt him. Though my father is a good man."

"You told me yourself they might kill you for running off like that."

"That's different. They can kill me and still be good people."

He regarded her. In that statement, there were maybe several thousand years of context. *Fuck context*, he thought. He didn't know what to say to her. He silently watched her until Nasser walked into the room. His eyes were puffy and bloodshot; he'd been drinking heavily all the time lately. Issa signaled him to come closer. He switched the web page back to the burned women. As he did, Mehran also popped his head in behind Nasser.

"Take a good look."

"What am I looking at?" Nasser asked.

"Read, you whore's son." He grabbed Nasser's hand and pulled him closer to the computer screen. See these women? They all burned themselves. Do you know where? Down where my people come from. That's where. Do you know why? Because their *kiri* husbands, people such as yourself, wouldn't stop beating them. Every seventeen days. Do you know what that means?"

Nasser looked embarrassed, and with Hayat, whom he didn't really know, standing next to him. He said a noncommittal "no" and made to leave the room.

Issa pulled him back. "Read, you bastard."

"I don't beat women." He gestured toward Mehran. "He's not a woman."

"What? You mean you are going to beat him until he agrees to become a woman and then you'll stop? Nasser, what has happened to you?"

"If you want to fight, we'll fight right now."

"I don't want to fight you. And Mehran over there is not getting an operation to make you feel better. Do you understand? If you want to marry a woman, go marry a woman."

They all turned and looked at Mehran, who was standing by the door of the room. Now Aziz, too, pushed past Mehran and came inside. She surveyed all of them, and finally settled her focus on Nasser. "Did you beat this man? Look at his face. You beat him?"

"I don't know you. What do you want?"

"Did you beat him?"

Issa answered, "Yes, he did."

Aziz came right up to Nasser, stared him in the eye, and then delivered a ferocious slap. "You hit anyone again, I will send you to your grave."

And there they were—Issa, Hayat, Nasser, Aziz, and Mehran. In a room that had seen so much grief in another time, and where it now felt like everything was on repeat. They all waited. There was a moment when Issa thought Nasser might lose it and attack everybody there. He still had his hand around Nasser's. Now he hardened the grip. But Nasser wasn't moving. The firehouse captain stared at Aziz for a moment, turned back to Issa, peeled away Issa's grip slowly, and stepped out of the room and then the apartment without looking at anyone.

Finally, Aziz addressed Issa, breaking the silence. "Son, I already know this young man's story," she said, pointing to Mehran. "Hayat told me. Men are destroyers. And now I am going to make some tea and breakfast for all of us, because you have more troubles."

"What troubles, Nana?"

"Hayat will tell you."

With that, she and Mehran left the room.

Hayat said, "We came here last night because the doctor came back around."

"Madam Doctor's husband?"

"Former husband."

"With the big guy? The bodyguard?"

"Two of those big men this time."

"What does he want?"

"He wants the mother of his child, Madam Doctor. And if he does not get her he will hurt Aziz, he said."

Issa's gaze shifted from Hayat back to the computer screen. "What do you want me to do?"

"I do not wish that I were in your shoes, Mr. Issa."

"I need more wisdom from you than this, young Hayat."

"Madam Doctor must marry Mr. Jafar immediately."

"You think they love each other?"

"They care for each other. One can see. This is an excellent beginning."

"What about you?"

"I would like to marry Ramin one day. As for you, you must keep Mr. Nasser from hitting Mr. Mehran."

"You cannot marry Ramin. His papers still declare him a woman. He has to be certified as, well, a guy. I don't make the rules, the government does. Ramin can't just promise the Ministry of Health that he'll get the surgery at some future date and take your hand in the meantime. He must actually get it, the penis, and then follow with all the legal stuff—name change, certificate of past exemption from military service as a current man and former woman, all that. It's a process. It doesn't happen in a week or a month. Understand? It's how things work in this country."

"You are very lonely, Mr. Issa."

"Jesus." Issa sighed.

"Yes, Jesus."

"What about Jesus?"

"Well, your name, Issa, it means Jesus. You are named Jesus, Mr. Issa."

"Thank you. I am often reminded of that."

After she was gone, he texted Jafar: Trouble here.

Jafar wrote back: *I am aware. Madam Doctor's mother called her.*

But this eye surgeon has picked the wrong fight. He knows people. I know more people.

You will handle it?

Haven't I always?

How come you'll handle it?

Meaning what?

Are you in love with Madam Doctor?

Let's not get ahead of ourselves.

Just tell me.

I read her a poem.

Issa waited for him until he wrote it out in the next text. *"Kind stranger, should you pass my house / bring light, and a window / through which I might gaze at the lucky street."*

He wrote back: Reciting a poem is all it takes?

No, Issa jaan. But we have to start somewhere.

It was a bit quick, though.

I'm almost a cripple. I don't have time. I need someone. Even you said it.

And what does Madam Doctor need?

Protection.

It wasn't the whole story. But it was a start. Jafar was right. He remembered that old poem that Jafar had recited to her. Probably Jafar and Commander Massoud had at one time also recited it to each other prior to some battle up in the Hindu Kush mountains.

Thirteen hours later he'd be on the train toward the province that had the highest number of burned women in the whole country. He'd speak to Aziz before leaving. "Listen, Nana, my friend Jafar will look after you and Solmaz until I get back. I won't be long."

"Where are you going?"

"Women burn themselves, Nana. Did you know that?"

"Yes, it is what we do."

"No, I don't mean like in the kitchen when they are cooking. I mean, they really burn themselves. They get fed up and they pour something on themselves and light a match."

"Listen, boy, I am a woman who was burned a long time ago. No one can touch me more than they already have."

"I know that, Nana. You're strong. But my friend Jafar . . ."

"Yes, yes. I know. He will make a couple of phone calls and the bad doctor will turn into a little mouse and go away. I know how these things work."

And Jafar would. It was the burning, though, that unraveled him. A woman like Aziz can look him right in the eye and tell him she was burned a long time ago. If Aziz can say that, what about everybody else? He really had no idea what he meant to do in the south, whom he wanted to see, and what he'd accomplish.

Maybe he was being childish. But he was going. No way around that. He thought of another poem, an English poem called "The Waking." It had sat in their shelves in one of Hashem's collections of modern poetry. The last line went: *I learn by going where I have to go*. At some point, years later, upon arriving at that poem, Issa saw that Hashem had crossed out the word *learn* and instead, over it, he'd scribbled the word *go* in pen: *I go by going where I have to go*.

He favored Hashem's line over the original.

Fourteen

Godarzi said, "Agha Issa, why do you want to see this family? They've had their pain, now they should be able to go on with their lives."

"How can they just go on, after everything that happened?"

"Agha Issa, we haven't seen you in, what, twelve years? And suddenly you want to know how people here manage to endure? Yes, they go on. My daughter, *alhamdulillah*, she made it to college, studying to be a pharmacist. But if she had burned herself, what should I do? Kill myself?"

"But you didn't make your good daughter want to burn herself in the first place, Godarzi *jaan*. There is a difference."

"You think the family is responsible? I know them. I know the father. He's a good man. Plays sad songs and happy ones on his *ney*. They're just poor farmers who don't know any better. Nobody beat that girl, as far as I know. You come back here with your city ways and you want to teach them what? And where have you been, anyway?"

"I went across the waters of the world, Godarzi *jaan*."

"And what did you find there?"

"Nothing."

They sat outside one of Borujerd's famous old ice cream shops. After failing as a farmer, Godarzi eked out a meager living driving around the occasional domestic tourist. He bit into one of two huge ice cream sandwiches on his plate.

"That thing you drink, Agha Issa, looks evil," Godarzi said, gesturing to Issa's espresso.

"Tastes it too."

"Why drink it, then?"

"The bitterness of life must be remembered every day."

"The waters of the world have turned you mad. Khoda rest your brother's soul. And your father's."

Their old man would sometimes bring Issa and Hashem to these ancestral lands to toughen them up. The old man bragging how his own father used to bring him back here and release him to the care of the nomadic tribes during their summer migrations to the highlands. It was the same old thing, Hashem failing at sharpshooting and all the other things that male members of the Lor tribes were expected to excel at. They'd spend two weeks with extended family in the hilly villages above Borujerd, where they would presumably learn to become men. Issa had loved every minute of it, and Hashem had despised it. The saying in Iran went that a Lor was quick to go for a stone or piece of brick. It wasn't untrue. More than once, Issa had seen a perfectly peaceful afternoon in the village go south in the time it took to drink a cup of tea. It wasn't fighting simply to put another man in his place. If the fighting started, and it always did, then it was for blood, and it often ended in someone getting killed. It was a carnival of fierceness that was bound to honor and loyalty, and you couldn't explain or make an outsider believe it until they saw it with their own eyes. It was the stuff of myth, more often than not as ugly as it was breathtaking. It was a state of permanent war. And it was here, to his home, that he had returned to find out why women were burning themselves.

Godarzi said, "This thing you've come here to find out, what will you do with the knowledge?"

"Nothing. I'll just know."

"You'll just know? Well, I can tell you why our young women are burning themselves. Because they are treated poorly."

"You just said the farmer we're going to visit is a good man. Now you say he isn't?"

"I did not say he is bad. Do not put words into my mouth. Besides, if you want to see cruelty like that, why come here? Why not go to Dishmook?"

That was the place where self-immolations occurred every seventeen days.

"I don't know anyone in Dishmook. But I know you here. No one would talk to me if I went there."

"You are a soft Lor, Issa. And your brother was no Lor at all. May he and his softness rest in peace. Your poor father. His sons turned out to be questionable Lors."

Issa's phone buzzed. There were multiple messages. From the language institute, wondering why he had simply not shown up to teach that day, not for the first time. Nasser had been calling him too. Five missed calls.

But now it was an unknown number calling, the area code from farther south. He left Godarzi to his ice cream for a minute and strolled down the spacious boulevard. He imagined himself living here, in this town full of ancestors with their famous ice cream, excellent kebab, and hot tempers. By the time he answered the call it was too late. There was a message.

I beg you to pick up. It's me, Ramin. I'm using someone else's phone.

It was trouble. He'd expected it. First, though, he had business with his own people right here on the outskirts of Borujerd.

THE FARMER SAT on the floor against the wall of the long room where they all ate and slept. It was a poor setup, like that of many farmers around here. You could smell manure from the kitchen on the other side of a high wall. A loud TV was set to some foreign satellite channel in a language that Issa didn't recognize. Two twin boys sat in front of the screen and gazed at huge men trying to lift various objects above their heads while screaming at the top of their lungs. The twins would imitate what they saw and then roll into a wrestling match across the threadbare carpet. It lent the room a level of insanity that was only somewhat balanced by the movements of a quiet girl of about ten who separated the twins, served her father tea, and then went back to lending her mother a hand in the kitchen.

Godarzi had dropped him off here after talking with the father. He was supposed to return in two hours.

The father smiled. "You write for the newspapers?"

"I want to thank you for your time." He had the cash ready and delicately left it next to one of the big pillows by the wall so that the father could see it. The twins screamed again, and the father's attention went to them for a minute.

"Godarzi said your people are from around here."

"Yes. I'm a Lor. Like you."

The boys now tumbled their way toward the father. He laughed and let them wrestle. One of the boys knocked into a tray in front of the father, sending his rolling tobacco every which way. The girl came back from the kitchen, shouting at the boys to stop. But they wouldn't let up. Now they climbed on top of the father, crawling across his chest and onto his shoulders. The girl saw the money Issa had left by the wall, picked it up, and smiled at her father, who smiled back.

"Give it to your mother."

He had expected the man to make a show of not accepting the money. But there was something tired and resigned about the fellow. He did not make false protests. For a moment, Issa was grateful to the twins, for their energy and the way they filled the air with their little universe. Why had he even come here? The newspaper report about this man and his family and the burned girl, just turned fourteen, had noted she had been the top student in her class in the village. To attend high school, she'd have to take the bus into town, to Borujerd and back, every day. When they'd interviewed the father, he'd said he had a bad back, a broken back he called it, from a tractor accident some years earlier. He needed her on the farm, and why did a girl need to go to school past a certain age anyway? He had sounded matter-of-fact, curious, not vicious—not like someone who would beat his fourteen-year-old daughter.

As the twins' attention was again diverted by the television, their father hunched over, gathered the tobacco from the carpet, and fixed the tray.

"We are poor folk, Agha Issa, forgive us if we cannot offer you much. But you must stay for dinner. I asked Godarzi to join us too. We have meat."

The phone call to the number Ramin had left him distracted Issa, and he kept going back to it. Not only had Hayat's family not said yes to the marriage proposal, which Issa had been certain they'd refuse, but Hayat's brothers had then proceeded to give Ramin a severe beating, demanding to know where Hayat was. This much he'd gathered after the phone conversation. The rest, though, was vague, because in fact it wasn't Ramin who he spoke to but the man, the cousin to whom Hayat had been offered in marriage.

"Mr. Issa, I would like to bring this . . . person to Tehran and have a talk with you."

Standing on the street in front of that ice cream shop in Borujerd, all Issa could muster in response was that he wasn't in Tehran but much farther south, in fact only a few hours' drive from their town; perhaps they could instead catch up the next morning. Issa had suggested they meet at the ice cream shop in Borujerd proper.

"Are you unwell, Mr. Issa?"

He turned his attention back to the Lor farmer, who was rolling a cigarette and looking at Issa with genuine concern. He recalled a Thomas Hardy novel he'd read in terrible Persian translation years ago. The family is so poor that the oldest child decides to kill himself after killing his siblings, so that there are less mouths to feed. Such a dubious and melodramatic way to end a novel, and he hadn't believed it for a minute. Now he wondered if he hadn't been mistaken. Maybe folks really did kill themselves over such things.

He realized he knew nothing. Here he was, facing this man whose daughter had crisped herself and left behind a note that said she had wanted to become a doctor. A doctor, like Solmaz. Melodramatic? What if Issa's old man had not forced Aziz to put Solmaz in school way back then? What if his old man hadn't grabbed Solmaz's hand that fateful day and taken her to school to enroll her in first grade? One day, three months in, Solmaz came to the apartment and locked herself in the bathroom. She refused to emerge. At school, someone had said she was merely a maid's daughter. A servant girl. She was humiliated. They had found her out. After Aziz screamed at her daughter from behind the door, the old man stood patiently there for a half hour speaking gently to Solmaz, telling her how special she was and how one day she would show everyone her true worth. Which part of this was melo-dramatic? It was life. He had been mistaken to come here. This soft-spoken farmer with the bad back whose other daughter had just given him a kiss on the cheek had to live with that suicide note for the rest of his days. Everything was wrong. Nasser was wrong. The eye surgeon was vile. And the world was as *kiri* as it could get.

"Your daughter?" Issa could barely get the words out.

The farmer suddenly stood up and took Issa's hand. "Come."

They had to pass through the kitchen, where the mother and the girl were hard at work making the evening's dinner. He heard the woman offer words of thanks and praise, something vague about the money and how they did not deserve it at all.

He lost the thread. This farmer leading him off to the back

somewhere, past the outhouse and the single cow in the pen they owned. Past their Persian cucumbers and Persian melons, and he knew what was coming and cursed himself for being here. Who was he to judge anyone? Alexander the Great had gone through this geography—maybe right through another iteration of this village—on his way to burn down Persepolis. History was full of blazes. The mighty Persian Empire singed by a young Greek immortal.

A shiny piece of stone with flowers on it. The farmer kneeled, said a prayer, looked up at Issa, and started crying. Life. Right here in the Lorestan province of Iran, where self-immolation happened to be in vogue among girls of a certain age. They hardly had bread to eat, but they had their cell phones and gave pointers to one another on social media on how to go about killing themselves.

"I did not realize this is what she would do, Agha Issa. I swear on the Messiah, I didn't."

Issa sat next to him. "Why didn't you bury her at the cemetery?"

"A curse on all of them. Some mullah started to say something about suicide and this and that." The farmer looked away and then began rearranging the flowers. "You know what I did? I spit on them. That is what I did. I spit and walked out. Then I buried her in the mountains. But I buried her notebooks right here in a small box. So she can be next to us always. Every day I come here and pay her a visit. Khoda broke my back twice. Once on the tractor and once with my daughter. That girl was the light of my days."

"Then why did you not let her continue with school? Why drive her to this? I am sorry to ask you the question."

"Are you really from the newspaper?"

Issa took awhile to answer. A flock of sheep hurried down the road.

"No."

"Why come here, then?"

Issa told him: he had wanted to know what kind of a man would let his daughter burn herself.

"I am not that kind of man, Agha Issa. There are evil men right here in this village. You and I can take a walk and I can show you which men are evil. Men who take the bread right out of their daughters' mouths. Men who have the fires of hell in their eyes. I know them. But I am not that man. I just told her to help around the house for a year until I got better and then she could go back to school if she wanted to. And then she goes and burns herself."

The farmer burst into tears again and then began hitting himself on the head hard enough to cause Issa to restrain him.

"I'm sorry. I shouldn't have come."

The farmer stopped. "I am glad you came. I am afraid, Agha Issa. What if my other daughter . . . what if all the daughters of Lorestan want to burn themselves? What then?"

NASSER SHOUTED INTO THE PHONE, "I can't find Mehran. "Where is he? You know where he is. Tell me. I accept—Mehran, not Mehra."

Godarzi was working on a plate of ice cream. A police van pulled up and five uniforms sat around a long table a little ways down, eating platefuls of the same. It was pitch perfect, peaceful. The Orient, disingenuous in its innocence, dilapidated, picturesque. Two of the policemen were doing their mandatory service.

It was usually easy work, policing as a recruit. Though not always. Issa's own military service had been anything but easy. One time during a demonstration, his unit had been called in for crowd control. He'd waited in an unfriendly town in an unfriendly province and wondered if and when it came to it and a dozen angry men attacked him, what level of violence he would have to resort to. It didn't take long for him to find out. There, in that no-name place in Kurdistan, incensed men raging at him like that. They wanted something from him. What? He was just a soldier doing his job. And his job at that moment was to do violence. Because this was the lingua franca they all understood. His baton had connected with the first man, and when the second man tried pulling it away from him, Issa delivered the kind of kick his old man would break thick wooden boards with during pointless karate demonstrations.

Back at the barracks, they'd treated him like a hero that day. They weren't celebrating him; they were celebrating their own survival, and somebody had to be their point of focus. He thought: *Live long enough and you might even stand over your daughter's fake grave in the back of your own house.* He had asked the farmer if this time around he'd let his other daughter finish high school. *With Khoda, who punishes me, as my witness, this one is going to become a doctor if I can help it. A real Madam Doctor.*

"You fool, Nasser," he spoke into the phone. "You have finally managed to scare Mehran away from you."

"No, I want to marry him. See, I am accepting him as Mehran. Are you happy now?"

It was like talking to a child. "You cannot marry another man in this country. Where do you think you are?"

"You see? My point exactly. If he were a woman—"

"Let's not go there, all right?"

"Where is he?"

Issa didn't know. Everywhere in the neighborhood there was war, figuratively and literally. In any direction you could get lost in death's maw. Yes, he, too, was worried for Mehran, but not that worried. If Mehran could survive this long in a city like Tehran, he could also survive Nasser. The Nassers of this geography were always at the threshold of some emergency anyway. Maybe that was why Nasser was a fireman. It suited his character.

Like how Jafar suited Solmaz, as she did him. He understood that more and more now. Jafar had already sent a follow-up message. The eye surgeon had been quick to dispatch goons to Madam Doctor's office too. *I'm having the situation taken care of like I said I would. He won't be doing anything like this again. You can be sure of it.* A steely determination in Jafar's note that Issa hadn't sensed in a long time. The kind of determination that reminded him of his friend's years of karate at the dojo and the years of combat in Afghanistan that followed.

He would have liked to say a big fuck you to Nasser just then and hang up. Instead, he played nice. "We'll find Mehran together. I promise. He can't be far. I will be back in Tehran tomorrow."

Godarzi was staring at him strangely. "Agha Issa, what man marries another man?"

Issa looked askance at Godarzi.

"I'm sitting right here. I heard you speaking on the phone just now."

"It happens."

"First, you come here looking for the family of a burned girl. Now this? What happened to you across the waters of the world?"

When Issa was a kid, this was the man who would sit him on a donkey and have him ride for hours through the upland villages. It was before Godarzi had his own children, and he treated Hashem and Issa as if they were his. But now they'd reached the shelf life of their clan's patience. He could see it in good old Godarzi's eyes. Godarzi was, unlike most Lors, not one to get angry too quickly or show it. But the anger was there now, in the swell of the fellow's voice, in the way he looked at Issa as if a primordial contract between them had been defiled.

Issa tried being philosophical with the man, knowing very well it would get them nowhere. "Godarzi *jaan*, the world, its waters and its ways, are bigger than Lorestan."

"So?"

So nothing. There was little left to say between them. His faith in a fellow Lor gone for good, Godarzi said good-bye and left Issa to sit alone the rest of that September afternoon in Borujerd, until Ramin and his ride finally showed up at the ice cream shop— Ramin's face battered and looking illicit, like something wrecked on purpose or anchored incorrectly, his gaze resting on Issa like an inquisition.

ISSA REMEMBERED HASHEM'S very last play. It was about illness. Hashem's own illness. The actor playing the role of the sick man had come from the deep south of the country. A young Black man from the Gulf who, like Hashem, was dying. He was slender and small, a boy really. His voice a brass of resentment against bad luck. He had been accepted to the University of Tehran as a theater student and had eventually found his way to Hashem and his band of actors. Dark-skinned and dying—a combination that invited commentary. Once, right after a performance, Issa had heard a man in the audience say, "Black *kaka* knows how to act. We could use him for bit roles in television."

A few minutes later, Issa cornered the man outside and applied a rudimentary choke around his neck. "You wish to repeat what you said inside?"

People were no fucking good. But you couldn't hammer virtuousness into them. And who were you to even try? But you could make them eat their bad behavior now and then, whether outside of a theater or under the Hafez Overpass. Sometimes it was you who were no good; you who were just a soldier serving in the wrong place at the wrong time, so that when the call came to crush a demonstration because people were sick and tired of eating shit, you beat them with a baton or kicked them like an animal because you had convinced yourself there was no other choice, that you were just another miserable conscript putting in your time, and if the world had been different, well, you'd have acted with more civility toward it.

The sick actor from the Gulf had ended up dying nearly a year before Hashem, his wasted body a store of bruises toward the end. His last role had had a withering refrain, sounding like a broken record: "Nurse, why is it so cold in here?" A question he'd uttered exactly twenty-three times in the play. Issa had counted.

What had been the actor's name? He couldn't recall, and probably Ramin, who lay on the adjacent bed in the fleabag guesthouse in Borujerd, did not know either. The established hotels would have all required an ID from Ramin, whose official papers still designated him a woman. They'd pretended he'd lost his wallet in a fight; the shady guesthouse manager couldn't care less anyway. There was one miserable room available with a broken overhead fan and the drip-drip of a faucet reminding Issa of that dead actor's refrain. Violence and sickness and secrets, he thought. And Ramin lying next to him, with a face that resembled a squashed tomato, in this clammy room in the heart of the Lorestan province.

He called to Ramin to see if he was awake.

"I'm sorry," Ramin answered.

"Sorry for what, dearest?"

"For getting you into this. Issa *jaan*, maybe you should marry Hayat for now, and when, well, I'm official, you can divorce her and I'll marry her."

Issa started laughing. It was tired laughter, mirthless. "Do you know how ridiculous we are?"

"It's this culture that makes us ridiculous."

Culture, *farhang*, whatever.

At the ice cream shop, the man who'd accompanied Ramin had seemed gentle. He wore round-rimmed glasses and had on the unlikely combination of a suit and flip-flops. Indeed, he was Hayat's longtime suitor and first cousin, but he no longer wanted to marry Hayat. "I hope someone will, sir," he added, before turning back toward his car.

Issa stopped him. "Wait. Why are you doing this?"

"*That*," he said, pointing to Ramin sitting on a bench in front of the ice cream shop, "came to the door of my dear Hayat's family and asked for her hand. Hayat's people asked that thing to enter their home and then her brothers—my cousins—started to beat the miserable shit, thinking that was a man. Then they suddenly stopped, and now I know why. I was called to their house and was told this was shame. Shame beyond words. But no one knew what to do with this shame, and this . . . this thing. My cousins took the wallet to look for identification. Then, well, one of the sisters checked more closely, you understand. And you know the rest."

All of this information had been relayed with the car engine running and the man sitting behind the wheel looking dead ahead and not at Issa, as if he had stared into the eyes of Satan itself and all he wanted now was to get away as soon as possible.

He went on. "The brothers, my cousins, didn't even want to call the police. It was luck that they called me. This situation was beyond them. Who can call the police about something like this? What does one say to the police? It is a disgrace for them, for me. For everyone. Your friend there would be in the bottom of the Karun River right now, and nobody would have asked a second question. Do you understand?" He turned to Issa for the first time.

"I understand. And I thank you for saving my friend there. He has a name. His name is Ramin."

The man hiccupped and pretended to spit. "Ramin? I am not a fool, sir."

"Whatever you say. The law allows it; the Imam himself passed a fatwa allowing sex changes. In any case, I am grateful to you for bringing Mr. Ramin here to me. Hayat thanks you too."

"I do not want to hear from Hayat ever again. Do you hear? I do not want her to ever call her family. It would be a very bad idea. I saved this person sitting over there from sure destruction because Hayat was my everything. But I cannot marry her now. She is . . . I don't know what she has become. But I still cannot let our family harm Hayat either. We grew up together, all of us. She was the heart of my heart. And then she goes and runs away, and next this person calling themselves Ramin shows up. What is a man supposed to do? You tell me. Please tell me. I am a simple man and I want to know a few things in this world."

"You are a good man."

"A good man," the fellow repeated. "I told the family not to dip their hands in blood. I told them this was as much my affair. I would handle it as I saw fit. I put your friend in the car. I asked your friend to call someone. And we came here to meet you. I don't know who you are and I don't want to know. But tell me this: is Hayat safe with you?"

"Yes."

"You will protect her in Tehran?"

"Yes."

"Did our Imam really pass a fatwa sanctioning this? It is possible?"

"Yes."

"What does Hayat do until then?"

"I have her living with my nana. She will be taken care of, on the honor of my Lor ancestors."

"You are from this town then?"

"My fathers have been here since time began. Khoda be praised."

"A Lor is not supposed to know such things. Nor an Arab like me. We are different men, you and me. No?"

"The world is changing. If the Imam can see that, so can you and I."

The man sighed. "But I don't like it. I have a right not to like it."

"Yes, you have that right, my brother."

"Take care of Hayat. We don't ever want her back in Ahvaz. Understand? Her brothers do, but only to wash their shame with her blood. Keep her far away and protect her, please. I will find another woman to marry." He shifted into gear and stretched a hand toward Issa.

"*Allah yasalmak*, my brother," Issa said in Arabic, and pressed the man's extended hand. "Your cousin stays under my protection. And you have my number."

"I will erase your number. Good-bye."

He watched the Arab man drive away, back toward the Gulf and to the bubble of his fathomable world. Between them, Issa and that Arab man had preserved something for Hayat and Ramin, maybe even life itself.

Yet he felt nothing, not even relief.

He shouldn't have celebrated with the rest of his unit back in Kurdistan all those years ago. No one in the unit could take him on. They had nicknamed him Bruce Ali, after Bruce Lee, and during fistfights off the barracks, it was always Issa who was pushed ahead of the platoon and had to set their adversaries straight. The fighting was relentless; always there, a drug really. Or an animal that always followed you. Never quite letting you out of its sight. He would have told the old man who was so disappointed with him, *You see? I didn't need your shit-colored black belt to make it in the world.*

Still, he shouldn't have celebrated after thrashing those Kurdish men.

Now he reached over to the other bed in the flophouse room and touched Ramin's shoulder lightly.

"What is it, Issa?"

"I was thinking, you are not a man yet."

"Yes, I am."

"Then why are we in this room and with you looking like a truck ran over you?"

"Because we were born in garbage and in garbage we live."

"I disagree."

"Suit yourself. And take your hand off me."

Issa did. Such disquiet in this dank room with its broken everything.

"What were you thinking just now, Issa? That you would sleep with me tonight as some kind of achievement?"

"This is not generous of you."

"No. But it's the truth, isn't it? We're here in this room, and you wanted to put one down in your notebook for the ages, right? Issa sleeps with Ramin. Fuck you, Issa. I'm not stupid."

"Well then, what if I marry Hayat?"

"Now you are just being mean and vengeful. Hayat and I love each other. And you don't even love Hayat. You are still searching for love, stupid."

With a sigh, Issa got up and went to the toilet and stuffed a sock over the mouth of the leaking faucet. The noise stopped, and its stoppage made the silence that much more unbearable. Then he came back into the room. "I'm sorry."

"I know you are." Ramin lay perfectly still on the bed, his eyes following the wobbly fan above them. "You are just trying everything you can think of. That's all."

"What does that mean?"

"You think of love as something to be found. There are men

like you. And women too. Since I've been both, I know. Love is not something you find. Maybe it is, actually. I'm not sure. I guess I just feel sorry for you."

Hovering over his bed, Issa suddenly noticed Ramin's extreme discomfort. "Why are you sweating so much?" he asked.

"I feel horrible. I'm sick."

"Of course. You just took a terrible beating."

"It isn't that. It's the quality of the testosterone in the market lately. Can't get the European kind anymore. Nor the Canadian. Just some cheap stuff from who knows where."

"Why go through all this?"

"Why? Let me ask you this then: why search for love at all?"

"They're not the same thing."

"Perhaps not. But every search is important to the searcher."

Issa reached over again and this time held Ramin's wrist. He felt for the pulse. Ramin let him. Two men in a crappy room in nowhere Borujerd, Issa's ancestral home, holding hands and gazing at each other as nothing more than two souls with dismantled pasts.

"Why did you say you feel sorry for me?" Issa asked.

"You are alone."

"That can be fixed. Don't worry over me." He asked if Ramin knew where Mehran had disappeared to.

"He goes to his hometown now and then. Rents a room, kind of like us tonight, and spends a couple of days watching his family from a distance. Just observes them. They have no idea. The town is on the way to Tehran. I'll call him. We can stop there tomorrow and pick him up."

Issa withdrew his hand. This time, Ramin reached over and

put his palm in his. "It's all right. Stay with me." He smiled. "I've had a rough day."

They were quiet for a while, then Issa asked, "Do you think of Nasser as a beast?"

"Because he beats Mehran? No, I don't think him a beast. Issa *jaan*, it took me a long time to figure out that I was really a man in a woman's body. I know it sounds trite, like I'm giving you a lesson. But it's true. It takes time to know who you are. And a lot of people, maybe most people, they don't ever find out. They just chase their tails being uncomfortable. Uncomfortable with themselves. With the world. With those they think they love. That's Nasser for you in short. He doesn't know who he is. Or, actually, he's just finding out. And he's confused. He's scared. So he strikes out."

"I agree. But you're still being too generous to him."

"What else do we have in our lives, Issa, if not our generosity?" Ramin pushed himself up, brought his face close to Issa's, and planted a kiss on his cheek. He lay down again.

"That was you being generous to me just now?" Issa asked.

"Yes. That was me being generous."

Fifteen

By the time he got to Solmaz's apartment in the Yousef Abad district, the throbbing in his ribs had subsided a little. People imagined fighting was an art. But really, it was controlling fear that was art, staying put when you wanted to run. And when Nasser had finally attacked him inside his own place—while Ramin, Hayat, Mehran, and Aziz watched—he decided not to talk his way out of it. It had to happen eventually.

Solmaz examined his face and ribs. "Nothing broken. You're lucky. That friend of yours is an animal."

"What exactly happened?" Jafar asked.

His old friend looked sound, all things considered. It was the only way to put it. He might not be able to practice karate for five straight hours like in the old days, but there was something sturdy again in his gaze after a long while. As if he had been refurbished. It was Solmaz's doing.

At the question, Issa burst into sobs. Right in front of the Madam Doctor and Jafar. Even as he began to bawl, he knew that their empathy for him would be for all the wrong reasons, and they'd imagine he was crying because of a silly fight. This made him angry—with himself, and with them.

He took the tissue that Solmaz offered him. "It's not what you guys think."

"What do we think?" Jafar asked.

"I'm just tired is all. Our country tires me . . . I have a question. You two are in love, yes?"

Both of them laughed at the question. It was easy laughter, as if they were laughing at their own child. Issa cheered up.

Jafar looked at Solmaz. "Are we?"

Solmaz only smiled.

"I mean," Issa went on, "how does it work? One day I come back to my place, the two of you are there and getting along swimmingly. Is that love at first sight?"

Solmaz answered, "No. But you get a feeling something could be possible, so you open yourself to it."

"And what is it that you saw in Jafar that made you feel that way?"

"Trust."

Jafar laughed again. "Thank you for acting like I'm not even here."

"Jafar, I need to know. I need something more concrete."

"But you and I already talked about this, sort of."

"Humor me. Just a little bit more."

Solmaz appeared embarrassed all of a sudden. She excused herself and went into the kitchen.

"What?" Jafar asked.

"I'm tired of just reading about love. I'm tired of love poems. I want—"

"You know you sound ridiculous, Issa. Do you think every love poem somebody wrote meant they were pining just then?"

"Well, they must have been pining at some point, no?"

"With the Messiah as my witness, you are still a child, Issa."

Solmaz cleared her throat. She had stepped back into the living room and was watching the two of them. It was an awkward moment.

She said, "Every love poem ever written *was* written by someone who was pining—for something. But you don't always have to be in love to write a love poem."

Jafar sighed. "You two . . . are we going to have a debate on love poems now?"

It was a strange triangle, as if Issa were passing along a beloved or a child or a sister—or all of them at once—to someone else. It felt like sacrifice, even though it wasn't. The words to the poem Jafar had written to him came out instinctively, and he recited: *"Kind stranger, should you pass my house, bring light, and a window, through which I might gaze at the lucky street."*

Neither of them said a word. After a while Issa added, "You're each other's window now. Is that it?"

Jafar answered, "You might say that. Why not?" His voice was serious and even. Turning to Solmaz, he said, "Tell him."

"The two of us got married. We did it in Mashhad. Quickly and quietly. No family, no one. Just us."

Issa understood that they'd done it to shut the eye surgeon up once and for all. It made sense. Nevertheless, he said, "That was a bit fast, Madam Doctor."

"Sometimes fast is the only way."

"Congratulations, I suppose. Have you told Aziz?"

"Soon."

"And your former husband?"

"I told you I've already dealt with him," Jafar said decisively.

"Does this mean you can get Madam Doctor's boy back for her too?"

"He can continue to keep the boy, but he can't prevent Madam Doctor from spending time with her own son. This has been made clear to him. He will not be a problem again. To anyone."

What was it Ramin had said yesterday? *It's this culture that makes us ridiculous.* The similarities between Solmaz's and Hayat's trajectories struck him. An Arab girl from the far south and an Azeri Turk, a Madam Doctor with a thriving practice in the capital, and it still made no difference. They both needed protection. Because truly people were no good—and culture, fucking culture, you might as well take a piss on it.

He didn't have to ask what Jafar had done to shut the eye surgeon up. A call or two to former associates in the Guards and a carful of unforgiving men pay the surgeon a visit. It doesn't matter whom in the hierarchy of power the surgeon knows or whom he's performed cataract surgery on. The men do not rough up the surgeon, but the threat is there. The threat is everything. It is one of the lessons an officer in their unit had drilled into Issa: If you want to get information out of a guy, don't beat him right away. Instead, let the threat of the beating linger in the fellow's mind. Fear makes men start to sing.

But it wasn't enough. Somebody had to pay. Maybe the surgeon did. Or the man whose wife had burned herself. Maybe even Nasser. They had to know more than just fear. They had to know there was a price to pay for the things they did.

Jafar was asking him, "What will you do now? About this friend of yours, Nasser. Do you want me to have him dealt with too?"

No, he didn't want that. Nasser was his issue alone, no one else's. The fight they'd had, it was inevitable. Even as he was driving back to the capital with Ramin, he'd known that a face-off with Nasser was probably awaiting him. On the way, they'd had their driver stop in Mehran's hometown to pick him up too. What a sight they'd made in the back of that rental car, while the driver pretended not to notice Ramin's and Mehran's bruised and beaten faces.

And then it happened. Because it had to. There's Nasser, sitting on the couch, delirious. He has been waiting in Issa's house, refusing to speak to Aziz and Hayat, who are watching him. Who knows how long he's been here. Maybe minutes or hours or days. He must ascribe blame for what has happened to him, and the nest of all his troubles, he is certain, lies in this house. So he waits and waits. Nasser's jealousy is also pungent. It has a taste and a smell, and Issa can tell that the man has not washed in days. Nasser stands up and regards the three people who have just walked through the door—Issa, Ramin, and Mehran.

To Issa he says accusingly, "I thought you didn't know where Mehran was."

Issa decides to rile him, so they can get to the point and fight it out.

"What of it?"

The others say nothing. They also seem to understand that this, whatever it is, has to be worked through and become a part of their shared history. Nasser carries a quiet rage—none of the usual chest-thumping of his other fights—like an instrument that he's going to crush Issa's face with. When he gets within striking distance,

Issa sidesteps and kicks him cleanly into the dining table. The shock of it makes everyone freeze. It's a fleeting victory, and Issa knows that in the next few seconds he is going to be pounded to the floor. When it happens, when he is underneath Nasser and blocking his face to soften the blows, he senses that Nasser is holding back. The blows are hard enough, but they are not crushing blows. This surprises Issa. It's almost as if something, some authenticity, is being stolen from him. He wants to yell at Nasser to hit harder and faster. It's not a fight worthy of either of them.

"Do you like to fuck Mehran from the back, or do you like him riding you like you're riding me now?" Issa manages to bring out in between the blows he is receiving.

"Shut your fucking mouth."

"Or maybe it's a give-and-take."

"I'll kill you."

Nasser presses both hands into Issa's neck. To get a better grip, he has to almost bear-hug Issa on the ground. It's Issa's opportunity; he tries to reverse their situation by triangle-choking Nasser with his legs. It almost works. But then it doesn't. Nasser's neck is far too thick and Issa has not attempted this move in a long time. He fails.

But even in failure, there is another pause. Nasser is puzzled; he realizes he almost ate it just now. He pushes back on his man and is about to start pounding again when Aziz finally intervenes. It's her age-old intervention, tried and true. A whack at the back of Nasser's head with the frying pan. Nasser barely manages a sound, rolling off Issa and curling onto the ground with his head in his hands. He is obviously disoriented but still keeping it together. Anybody else receiving a blow like that would have to be taken to the hospital.

Aziz says to him, "Don't show up here again if you are going to be a beast."

Now Mehran reaches out for Issa. As soon as he pulls Issa up he slaps him right across the face. "Yes, I do like to ride Nasser, since you wished to know. That's how I like him to fuck me. Satisfied?"

Ramin and Hayat watch quietly from a corner of the room. Issa notes that they are holding hands. The whole goddamn world is holding hands. He looks over at his friend, Nasser, still on the ground, writhing in pain. And Aziz there, frying pan in hand. It's that ancient orange one she always used to use when fixing fried eggs with dates for Issa and Hashem.

Ramin comes to him with an ice pack, gesturing to Issa to apply it to the back of Nasser's head. The fireman does not resist the small kindness. He looks up at all of them. Untrained in the art of apologies, all he can manage to say is, "I don't want to be . . . gay."

Hayat steps forward and says to him, "Why not, Agha Nasser? What part of it bothers you?"

It's a simple question, but one that Nasser hasn't the depth to answer. He is a man who is attracted to another man. It is a level of perplexity that confounds him.

Ramin says, "Agha Nasser, you managed to turn a perfectly good thing with my roommate to shit."

"I'm tired. I want to go to sleep," he says.

"You can sleep here," Issa offers.

"I will break his head if he tries anything," Aziz warns.

Issa would like to believe that men don't turn things to shit, but rather they just wade through it. He plants a kiss on the back of Nasser's bruising head. The other man lets him. This could be a beginning, Issa thinks, or an ending.

Sixteen

The amphitheater turned into a chorus singing along to an old poem by a beloved Syrian poet. Issa imagined the famous Iraqi crooner onstage was singing directly to them and looking right at them, at Mehran in fact, who was up from his seat whirling with infectious abandon. Soon, just about all the women in their row were doing the same.

Afterward, strolling by the cafés at the *wadi*, Mehran asked, "Why did you really bring me to Lebanon?"

"I figured I couldn't find love here, maybe you would instead. This country is a ruin, but it's full of romance."

"Just not for you, Issa," Mehran teased.

"I'm not lucky that way."

"Why not?"

"I'm always betting on the wrong horse. I'm a donkey, after all."

"Oh, Issa." Mehran reached over and pecked him on the cheek. The cafés were full. A Christian town in the mountains halfway to Syria, the high autumn air fragrant and relaxed. It was good to be away from Tehran. The sound of Arab families speaking French hovered over the tables.

The two of them found a corner seat by the stream where a statuette of Mary Magdalene stood surrounded by flickering candles. After the *mezze* and *arak* was brought for them, Mehran reached for Issa's hand, like that first time at the language institute. It seemed like eons ago.

"Issa, it's so beautiful here. Thank you for bringing me. I could have never afforded a trip like this on my own."

"I figured you needed a break. From Tehran. From Nasser. From all the craziness."

"How do you afford it?"

"Afford what?"

"This. Bringing me here. Everything."

"I know how to make money when I need to. It's not so hard." Issa didn't elaborate.

"I'm sorry I slapped you. I'd like to make it up to you."

"How?"

It was dark in their corner. Waiters were busy with other tables as families enjoyed an evening out. Just then, Mehran reached over and kissed Issa on the mouth. Issa froze. The lips of another man on his in this Christian mountain town in Lebanon. What would his father say? *You've turned* kooni *just like your brother.* He didn't pull back. Mehran shuffled his seat a little closer, and with his free hand pressed the back of Issa's head into his. A lip was just a lip. The last person he had slept with was one of his professors back in New York. That was what, two, three years ago? He had written a far-too-obvious paper comparing the love poetry of Pablo Neruda to a modern Arab poet. She had taken him to lunch. Then dinner. Then her bed. Eventually, she'd visited him several times in the wee hours of the morning at the hotel. Babacar winking at him afterward. "Brother Issa, the flag of Islam has been planted again, yes?"

"Yes, Baba. It is our planting season."

He figured he'd been just exotic enough to that professor, as a Middle Eastern guy with sufficient culture to be fuckable. Or maybe she just wanted to slum it with a guy, any guy, working the graveyard shift in America. Maybe it was kindness, or genuine attraction. Whatever it was, he figured he couldn't go wrong comparing Neruda and the love poems of the Syrian, Nizar Qabbani.

"Earth to Issa?" Mehran unglued himself from him. "Are you there?"

"Sorry, you caught me by surprise."

"Issa, I'm trying to show my appreciation to you."

"By kissing me?"

"Why not? It's a legitimate form of thanking, isn't it?"

"Am I that pathetic?"

"All you straight men are pathetic."

"What about Nasser, then? Don't you love him anymore?"

"Of course I do. He gave me shelter. In a way. But then tried to make me a prisoner. There's something to be said for someone who wants to make you their captive."

"This is logic that I don't understand at all."

"Because you've never been me—Mehran. A *kooni* in a country such as ours."

"Is it really as bad as that?"

"Listen, I love Tehran. I love the theater world in Tehran. I care for the few friends I've had over the years. I care for Ramin a lot.

But no one had ever come forward to make me their wife until now. Nasser, without knowing it, gave me dignity. Then he fucked it all up. He failed. But I didn't. Which is why I'm here with you. And if you like, I'll sleep with you tonight."

"Just tonight?"

"Yes, Issa *jaan*. Just tonight. You're not the kind of guy who wants more than a one-night stand with a Mehran."

"What if I told you I've already had that experience?"

"Oh, aren't we with the times?" Mehran smiled, caressing Issa's face, "Well then, I guess you'll just have to have one more experience."

THE BAR WAS off a quiet street on Rue Clemenceau near the Hamra quarter where he'd rented an apartment for the rest of their week in Beirut. He had wanted to gift Mehran. He was not sure what that even meant, though he imagined it might entail being good to a guy you'd slept with just that one time in Mount Lebanon. Afterward, Mehran had wept. And Issa didn't know if the beautiful man was weeping for his faithlessness to Nasser or because he was happy. When Mehran tried to hold his hand again on the street in Hamra, Issa gently knocked it away.

"This may not be the Islamic Republic, but they still have laws. They can throw us in jail for that, if they want."

"You are being a Nasser," Mehran shot back. There was no humor in how he said it either, and the rest of that day and the days after there were no more attempts at hand-holding of any kind.

They'd traveled north to Tripoli, where Issa took him to the soap sellers' quarter in the souk and let Mehran go on a shopping spree. Then they doubled back all the way to the Israeli border, where Mehran did his best Marilyn Monroe imitations by the dividing wall while Issa took pictures. It felt like a honeymoon for the misbegotten, and twice when Mehran tried to kiss him again, back in their room in Hamra, Issa simply froze.

"You won't catch anything, you know," Mehran said.

What he might catch didn't scare him. He just didn't know how to explain any of it to Mehran. *I'm not sure if I slept with you because I'm still trying to make something up to my dead brother, or because I want to punch my old man in the gut.* He imagined Mehran might say, *How about you slept with me because you simply wanted to?*

Yes, he had brought Mehran here to give him a holiday, to show him that another life was possible, and that the world awaited if he could just get that emigration case approved from Australia, Canada, or wherever. On the fourth night he decided to take Mehran to a nightclub in the Gemmayzeh district and watched Mehran's eyes light up from such an abundance of male attention. By now, it was like taking your kid out to the playground. He was happy for Mehran, and at the end of the night when he suggested they go back to the Bardo in Hamra and finish the night more quietly, Mehran asked if he could bring his "new friends."

The new friends turned out to be a group of Italians, suggestively dressed and entirely attentive to Mehran. Especially one of them, Marco, who at one point had Mehran bite into a slice of watermelon while he took racy pictures. They communicated through an odd mix of Italian that Issa slightly understood from his knowledge of Spanish, and the Italians' passable English. In a corner of the bar, some kind of poetry recitation was happening. He left Mehran to his new friends and went to listen to contemporary recitations in Arabic, French, and English. People clapped. Fashionable and suave. This was the Middle East that might have been. But it wasn't. Not even now, here; it all seemed an impossible experiment that could blow up in their faces any minute, and he felt a bone-deep tiredness suddenly overtake him. Maybe he could go to a pharmacy and get better-quality testosterone for Ramin than what they could find back home. He doubted it. Random thoughts like that, mixed with the reality of what he'd had with Mehran these past few days, rushed at him. Their lovemaking had been passionate enough because he had worked himself into wanting to get it right once and for all. At one point, Mehran called him "Nasser" by mistake, and they'd both laughed it off after some initial mortification—embarrassed with themselves, with their situation, and with the acknowledgment that they were just two people floating in the sea of unrequited everything before they had to return to the savagery of Tehran again.

Issa glanced back at the table where Mehran and the Italians were singing and laughing and knotting their arms together through their wineglasses. Not wanting to be a killjoy, he offered them the widest smile he could muster and signaled he would be turning in for the night. The protestations were genuine but not insistent. He winked at Mehran and walked into the Beirut evening, heading toward the American University campus. Past the police station, he doubled back. Crossing one of the side streets off Cheikh Elias, he felt a heavy shoulder bump into him.

"How would you like to get beaten up?"

He had encountered enough bodybuilders in Monirieh to know what he had in front of him. Without wasting time or words, he stuck two quick thumbs into the man's eyes, making him scream and grab his face. As he fell into the stance for sweeping out the man's legs and sending him flying, two other figures emerged from a waiting car.

He pushed his adversary to the side and squinted to see better.

The men looked familiar.

"Go ahead, pray. We want to see how you pray."

"It's not prayer time," Issa said. "Besides, what if I don't pray or don't feel like it?"

They had sent the injured guy home. He recognized one of the two who had gotten out of the car from the time he was stopped in the Dahieh district on his last trip to Beirut. The two men looked at him with a mix of curiosity, a little distaste maybe, and a good amount of fascination. He didn't know what they wanted, and so he went through the motions of the prayer like he did every morning, though he recited three *rakats* instead of the two required for the morning prayer.

The man said, "Which prayer of the day is this supposed to be?"

"It's my morning prayer."

"Then you prayed wrong."

"There's no such thing as a wrong prayer."

"Blasphemy."

"Why do you need to know if I know my prayers?"

He already knew why. In the army, he'd encountered similar situations; you could actually test a man to get a closer read on him. How a fellow prayed, what specific words he emphasized, what he did with his hands and where he kept them, whether he used a prayer seal or not, how deeply he articulated the Arabic or if he articulated too poorly, all these things said a lot about him, about what he was, and, most important, what he was pretending to be. Issa just wasn't sure why they were testing him in the first place. He didn't know if they were playing him for their own amusement or for something more pointed. They didn't bother to answer his question either.

Issa went on, "Besides, Allah loves a subject who is attentive; wrong or right doesn't matter."

"Oh, so now you are an expert?"

"My grandfather was."

"Is that why you fuck boys?"

There was a long pause. What did they want? Something in their demeanor had shifted since he'd been searching for Hayat here back in the spring, and they'd thought him a lost, bumbling Romeo looking for love at the wrong address. They still treated him as a joke, but this time they would not dismiss him so easily.

He said, "Do you guys have nothing better to do?"

The one he hadn't seen before said, "This is what we do. It's our job. You came to Beirut five months ago with some dumb story about a poetess, and now you're shacking up with a guy who is about to fuck some Italians in Hamra. What's your game in Beirut?"

"I don't have a game. Mehran is my friend and I brought him here to take his mind off some things."

"So you are not fucking him?"

"That's my business."

"You want to get hurt?"

"I think you have already seen that it's not so easy to hurt me."

"You fight well. How come? Who trained you?"

"My father."

The two men looked at each other incredulously and laughed.

"Did you ever serve in the army?"

"Of course."

"And then you spent time in America. This much we know about you."

"So? Half the people from Lebanon live elsewhere."

"We're talking about you, not the Lebanese."

"What do you guys want?"

"We ask the questions."

"Is this some sort of recruitment?"

"We want to know who you are."

"A nobody who fucked a pretty boy one night in Mount Lebanon. It happens. Get off my back, please."

Amazingly, they did. He didn't bother asking how they'd found him. He also knew that a couple of calls to associates in Tehran would give them more than they needed to know about his military service, his old man, the dojo, his brother, his education, and even his relationship to a man like Jafar, who was in a way one of their own.

Driving around town the next day, they threw bits and pieces of his own history back at him. They were men who knew things, and they wanted you to know that they knew. He was comfortable with that. They were Nasser types. Tough. Bullies, really. But they liked him, even if by this point he was also something of a *manyouk* to them. Which meant exactly this: no matter whether they liked him or not, they had to maintain a level of disgust for him.

The guy he had hurt in Hamra showed up at some point during the day and gave him a seemingly friendly but substantial blow to the shoulder. Issa let him.

"Let us know next time you are in Beirut."

"What for?"

"So we can show you around."

"Tour guides are not really my thing."

They gave him a tour of the city anyway, told him he was all right, not a bad sort, and that they'd be waiting for him if he ever decided he wanted some real adventure. He couldn't tell if they meant this or if it was all some peculiar diversion for them. But it was clear they at least appreciated his basic grasp of Arabic, so they didn't have to rely solely on English. Issa went along with it, telling them his house was their house in Tehran. The big man said, "I'll come to that dojo of yours in Tehran and I'll go a round or two with you, kickboxing. But I won't wrestle a homo." They all laughed at that. And again, Issa accepted the blow.

Was this the life Mehran had? Always the butt of somebody's joke? The amusing fairy, a diversion. It all suddenly fell into place, the things Mehran had told him these months, and Ramin too. It wasn't even about living at the margins; it was having to live according to a grammar that was not yours at all. Today he understood his own brother, Hashem, far better than he ever had before.

He went back to the room in Hamra, but Mehran wasn't there yet. Their flight was early the next morning. At some point, on a lark, he went back to the Bardo and found them there, Mehran and the Italians. They cheered loudly when they saw him and gave him tight hugs, which he didn't shy away from.

Mehran said, "I was about to come speak to you."

"You're not coming back to Tehran. Is that it?"

"They say my visa is good here for another three weeks."

"You have money?"

"You know I don't, Issa *jaan*."

"I'll give you some."

"Don't." Mehran nodded in Marco's direction. "The boy is smitten."

"And Nasser?"

"He'll have a place in my heart always."

"Wasn't Marco curious why your face is still bruised?"

"He finds it sexy." He laughed. "But seriously, Marco doesn't ask those kinds of questions. It's one of the beautiful things about him. He's an architect, you know. He'll take me to Turkey next. He says he would even marry me and take me to Europe."

The Italians were talking boisterously among themselves. They were the life of the party in this bar. Issa remembered years ago Hashem had said to him he wished he were Italian. When Issa asked why, he said it was because they wear themselves beautifully. Maybe there was something to Hashem's observation. The Italians wore themselves beautifully, and the Persians tragically. Maybe it could work, he supposed, between this Marco and Mehran.

Still, he wondered if it was wise of Mehran to take the plunge so impulsively. But who is sure of anything? He didn't want to think about the logistics of any of this, and yet it was starting to feel, again, like he was giving a member of his own family away.

"Take care of him," Issa said to Marco in a poor approximation of Italian.

"Issa."

"Yes, Mehran *jaan*?"

"I know what you're thinking. What if this Marco guy leaves

me in the middle of nowhere? Or worse. What if, what if, what if? Am I right?"

"Well, yes. And all the other stuff. It's not so easy, Mehran *jaan*, to just up and move to Europe. Not for people like us, you know. They don't exactly want us there."

"But Marco wants me there. And how about I try at least? Even if it's just for a few months. Isn't it better than what I have back home?"

"I can't argue with that."

"So you bless me?"

"Always."

"Issa."

"Yes?"

"I love you, but I need a guy who will love me back. You're not a man who loves—I mean, in that way."

"I suppose not."

"So are you good with this?"

"More than good."

"You'll come visit us?"

"I'm not made for the world you're about to enter, Mehran *jaan*. The Eastern Mediterranean is about as far west as I'll ever go from now on." He laughed. "We'll always have Beirut."

"What will you say to Nasser when you see him?"

"I guess I'll have another fight with him."

"Be careful, Issa. And . . . thank you, *azizam*. For all of it."

Seventeen

I know you're getting off that plane.

Nasser's text message had reached him as soon as he touched down in Tehran and had phone service. Outside, Nasser stood waiting by his car.

"How did you know when I was coming back?"

"You forget I used to work in customs. If I want to find something out, I find out."

"Now what? We fight again?"

"I'm done with that. You left him there, in Beirut?"

There was no reason to explain anything. They drove in silence past the Imam Khomeini grand mausoleum.

After a while, Nasser asked the question, "You slept with him?"

"I did."

"You fucked him?"

"I think I already answered that."

"Maybe he fucked you."

"What's the point of this questioning, Nasser *jaan*?"

"I just want to understand."

"What do you want to understand?"

"Were you ever—are you—in love with him?"

Issa sighed. "Of course not. I took him on a vacation so he could see life away from this godforsaken place for just a little bit, and to also be away from you. I had not counted on him not coming back. Though now I realize I had hoped for it."

"But you also fucked him."

"It happens."

"Do you like men? Do you like me?"

"Shut up."

"I haven't seen you with a woman since I've known you. . . . Do you like me?"

"Let's say I do. So what?"

"You do not like men—I know that for a fact. Yet you took mine away from me and fucked him. I want to understand why."

"You hurt that boy. I wanted him to forget you."

"Has he forgotten me?"

"Never."

A half hour later they sat in a *kalle-pache* joint where Nasser got two orders of whole sheep's head.

"Nasser *jaan*, I'm not big on eating animal eyes and brains."

"You're going to shut up and eat with me. You can fuck my wife-to-be, but you can't eat eyes and brains? Then suck my dick and *kiramo bokhor*."

"Mehran wasn't your wife-to-be."

"Shut up and eat."

They did.

Then Nasser made his announcement. "I'm getting married.

One of those suitables my family identified that we saw together, I went for a second visit while you were gone."

"You're going to marry someone you don't love?"

"Who has love?"

"Well, for a while I thought you did. Until you started ruining it."

"I'm getting married and that's that."

"Should I feel sorry for this woman you are getting married to? Are you going to make her life miserable?"

"Why would I do that? Let me tell you right now: no woman is going to burn herself because of me."

"I hope not."

"By the way, you remember in Zamzam, that guy I was going to fight with? The one whose wife burned herself."

"What about him?"

"The whore's son, his house burned something awful. By the time our fire trucks got there, the place was just a shell. A fire had started and somehow the gas main blew up. Lucky it didn't spread to the surrounding buildings. They'll have to tear the whole thing down and rebuild."

Issa stared at his plate of sheep's brain and tongue. He was speechless, knowing full well what had taken place. A pair of eyes were floating in his plate. He wanted to vomit.

Finally, he asked, "Was anyone hurt? Was that bastard hurt?"

"He wasn't hurt. He wasn't even there. You know, they tried to pin it on me at first. But I was at the firehouse when it happened. More than fifteen people vouched for me. Then . . ." He trailed off.

"Then what?"

He snorted. "They tried pinning it on you. Little did they know you were in Beirut getting your *kir* sucked at the time. When they found out, it really ruined their day."

"So who are they blaming?"

"Who? No one. This is called comeuppance. The ghost of that poor woman burned the fucking place to the ground. And good for her."

Issa pushed his plate toward Nasser. "Take it."

"You sure?"

Nasser ate more slowly now. It felt like a reckoning. It was in the air of the *kalle-pache* joint that reeked like a slaughterhouse.

"Nasser."

"I'm listening."

"I never took you for going for men." Issa said it as softly as he could. The place was packed with truck drivers, cabbies, laborers. Tough street men on their way to their morning routines.

Nasser spoke quietly. "I was waiting for something. All my adult life I've been waiting, brother."

The last thing he had expected was for Nasser to be so candid. It threw Issa off.

"Why deny yourself so long then?"

"And do what? Take a loudspeaker and tell all of Tehran I'm *kooni*? Where have you been, friend? I live and work in Zamzam. When you took me to that theater, it felt right. That's about it. It happened. But afterward it wasn't so easy anymore. You understand?"

"I understand."

Nasser took another bite of meat and pushed the plates away. "You understand nothing."

"All right. I understand nothing. What now?"

"Nothing is nothing and *hichi* is *hichi*. We eat *kalle-pache*. That's all. . . . Here." Nasser stretched a hand toward Issa over the greasy table. "Give me a good solid handshake."

Issa extended his hand and they shook.

"Issa, tell me the truth. I was just some kind of bridge for that boy, for Mehran. Wasn't I?"

"And he for you. It happens."

IN THE MOONLIGHT, the man's burned house could have been the kind of trash-strewn empty lot you'd find in the city a quarter century ago, with alley cats the only sign of life. It was a space of ruin now, a square shell of its former self, sooty and fragmented, shards of glass and concrete precariously balanced over bits of furniture. At the same time, the buildings next to it stood perfectly intact. There was something obscene in this. Sinister. The way you'd see cities where a rocket hits one building but spares the one next to it. He knew that coming here, now, was a bad idea. If he were spotted, the game would be over.

And yet he risked it and came anyway. Not for the sake of seeing the burned building, but because he needed to know why the Afghan foreman did it.

"Because when a woman burns herself . . . the world ends."

They were sitting in the same half-finished room as before, the foreman prepping a cut of opium over his brazier by rubbing it lovingly between thumb and forefinger.

He said to the foreman, "I've heard that sentence before. Did you learn it from Agha Nasser?"

"Who is Agha Nasser?"

"Never mind."

"It's something my uncle used to say. Back in Afghanistan."

"Why would your uncle say such a thing?"

"Why wouldn't he? The world is burning. Women are burning. Men are burning. I'm always burning. I was burning even before the Americans drove over my son. Afterward, I was just burned. Just like our supreme poet, Mawlana of Balkh, says—*sookhtam*. Understand this: one moment I was not burning; the next moment I was burned. There's a difference."

"Why did you do it?"

"Why do you ask, brother? You came here and told me what that man had done. We both knew what needed to happen in return. So I did it. No one knows, and no one shall ever know. Besides, when they decide to rebuild on that property tomorrow, they'll probably hire my team to do it. So I burned a place that needed burning. No one died. No one was hurt—I made sure of that. The man wasn't home at the time. And don't ask me how I did it. I know how to do these things. I'm an Afghan."

He offered Issa the opium pipe. Issa had once asked his old man if he'd killed anyone, maybe during his days as an officer in the military, or perhaps back in their ancestral lands where to fight and kill was as common as quenching your thirst. The old man would explain, more than once and maybe more than was necessary, that killing a man was one of the hardest things in life. Cutting a throat was hard. Strangling was hard. Only bullets were easy, but even those were hard. It wasn't as if this were cinema, the dojo master would say. Yet it was the way the old man said it that made Issa believe that in fact all these things were not so hard to do. Nor was burning a house so difficult. As he grew older and his belt colors changed at the dojo, the old man taught him how to take blows of every sort. *You have to learn to take a punch or kick before you can learn to deliver a true punch or kick. You have to learn what it takes to put a man down for five minutes or five months or five thousand years.* Issa had learned. Just as this Afghan foreman and one-time teacher had learned. There was some elegance in that.

The Afghan was speaking to him. "Don't think too much about it, brother. The poet says, '*God speaks to each of us as he makes us, then walks with us silently out of the night.*'"

Issa blew out smoke. "Did Mawlana Rumi say that too?"

"What did you call him?"

"Rumi. Did Rumi say that?"

"Why do you call Mawlana of Balkh by that stupid name?"

"It's how the rest of the world calls him."

"I saw good men die in my beloved Balkh. More than once. And I killed in Balkh. More than once. Do I care about a world that steals everything good we ever had? What if I were to call Mr. Rilke, Rilke of Balkh or Rilke of Kandahar or Rilke of Kabul instead? Would you be happy to hear that? The world only takes from us. They even rob us of our poets. The bastards."

"So we're back to Rilke."

"And why not? He was very wise and those words I just recited were in fact his. If I ever become a schoolteacher again I will teach his poems to my students—right alongside the poems of our great Mawlana of *Balkh.*" The foreman seemed for a moment to consider such a possibility: to be back in Afghanistan, a village full of kids in his ramshackle *madrasa*, and him reciting the words of the German poet. The idea was downright romantic and even miraculous—because it would never, ever happen. His country was beyond ruination. And the city of Balkh, too, was a place past redemption. The man took the opium from Issa, but instead of taking a hit, he began to choke up. "I recite these words every day of every year since my boy was killed: '*I love you more than all the fires that fence in the world.*'"

"Rilke again?"

"Let's just call him Rilke of Balkh for tonight. Is that all right with you?"

The two men sank into silence.

How did one go on living after losing a child and then being offered a measly hundred dollars for it? How many dollar bills would it take to even things out? He wondered about Mehran, over there in Beirut. Was it right to leave him there with strangers they'd just met in a club? And now, here. What was he after? Taking a cab straight to Zamzam was hardly the brightest idea. Yet there was no way around it; he had to know. He'd walked the last ten blocks so the taxi driver would not have an exact address of where he was going—just in case. The strangeness of it all. The ruin.

There were no cop cars on this street, no fire trucks, no busybodies trying to find out what had happened. Across the street was just another half-empty space that would be rebuilt tomorrow at an immense profit, or sold and then rebuilt. None of this would matter, and in the end he did not know or care what had happened to the man whose wife burned herself.

He murmured Rilke's name and asked the foreman if he could recite that bit of poetry in the original German.

"Now you are asking too much of me. I already burned a man's house for you. I cannot learn German or French for you too."

"That's fair. But do any of the men who work under you know what you did?"

"They are Afghans. Even if they know, which they don't, they do not know."

Issa breathed deeply and took back the pipe, relieved.

"You seem in deep thought, my brother."

"I have a friend, an African. A learned man like yourself. Yet he wants to come here to become a Shia cleric. Can you believe it? You and I may have not gone mad quite yet, but the world has."

"There were many Africans on the island they kept us on while I awaited my status. We were all waiting for a status. The whole world is waiting for a status, you know? But your friend is traveling in the wrong direction. He needs to be going to Europe. Maybe he lost his compass?" The foreman laughed quietly.

"Yes, I think he must have lost his compass."

"Or else you gave him the wrong compass."

"With Khoda as my witness, I did no such thing." They were quiet for a while. Then Issa asked, "Do you want some kind of payment for the favor you did me?"

"Do not insult me. It was a favor to myself. Men like the one across the street have made the lives of men like me rotten since before I can remember. I chose to do something about it."

"You know what the law will do to you in this country if they find out, right?"

"An Afghan who burns down a building? They would hang me. But only after a good many long beatings."

"And yet you still took the chance."

"Wouldn't you? Didn't you come here to do just that?"

"I wouldn't have had the courage you have."

"Yes, you do. If I had thought you haven't the courage, I would not have done you the favor. It is because I believed you have the courage that I took your place. This is called brotherhood."

He had spent a lot of money these past few weeks, especially in Beirut. Soon, though, he'd sell the dojo and his circumstances would improve dramatically. Also, he'd go back to work. He'd put together his own language school, a really, really good one. Maybe he'd hire this Afghan guy to teach Rilke. And Babacar had already written that his visa had come through. The big man was truly on his way now. First, he'd rid Baba of the preposterous idea of becoming a Shia cleric, and then he'd convince him to teach English and French and maybe even Arabic in their newly minted language school. Yes, the future was indeed radiant. He handed back the pipe and rifled through his pockets.

"What are you doing?" the foreman asked.

"I wish I had more, but this is all the money I have for now." He left the wad next to the opium.

"I said I didn't do it for money."

"Maybe money was just a little part of it. Yes?"

"Just a little. Thank you, my brother."

Eighteen

Babacar was to arrive in early December. What the West African was walking into was chaos. There had been street demonstrations. Suddenly everyone had turned into a dissident. There was too much enthusiasm and it was tiresome. Issa had been in demonstrations before, but as the soldier, and not just any soldier but one especially trained in the craft of dispensing pain. These demonstrations would go nowhere, he was sure; and even if they did, they'd eventually turn to shit because everything in these parts turned to shit and he was as guilty as anyone for that always happening.

Still, there was something inexplicably satisfying in the way Baba did not hesitate to head east. The big man was heading in just about the worst direction at a time like this—not unlike the Afghan foreman who'd returned home instead of rotting long enough on that Greek island full of refugees that some European door finally opened to him. Now and then Issa would recall the

Afghan and what he'd done in the Zamzam district. The burnings had come full circle. Justice was served.

But the streets of Tehran remained dark a lot of the time. In retaliation for all the protests, the internet was cut off. A pall fell over entire neighborhoods. Even language itself seemed to retreat. Issa opened an old compendium of poetry that his brother had left behind years ago and searched for one of the countless poems Hashem had put two check marks next to—that was what Hashem would always do: one check mark for something good, two check marks for a piece of literature he really, really liked, and three for the sublime. This poem was called "Losing a Language," and above the underlines from another life, Issa read: *many of the things the words were about no longer exist.*

So, yes, he'd start here. With language. But you couldn't just create a language school on a whim, not in Monirieh, not any-where in this city—even that business had its mafia. On the other hand, he had Jafar, the man with the connections, who immedi-ately put him in touch with the right folks and could give him the necessary clearances to turn the old dojo into a very different kind of school, instead of selling it. Jafar's name meant he would only have to give half the usual *baksheesh* to the men who'd be signing off on documents.

Meanwhile, the cities burned and riots flicked on and off and people still got married. Like Nasser, who had wanted Issa there at his wedding ceremony. Issa didn't go because Nasser was past tense, a violent language that he didn't want to return to anytime soon or really ever again. Though one day, passing by Daneshjoo Park, he noticed Nasser sitting behind the wheel of his parked car.

Issa hung back on the other side of the street and watched. After a while, a young guy came up to Nasser's passenger window, words were exchanged, and then the kid got into Nasser's car and they drove off. Nasser, who was married by then and newly settled in his Zamzam apartment with his new bride, was now seeking boys at the park. Under the radar. Nasser, in other words, had become predictable, like all men. He'd take his anger and his lust to the grave with him. He'd no longer fight for the honor of a burned anyone. And it was not impossible that he might one day drive his own wife to that very place. Though Issa doubted it; Nasser had an out now, Daneshjoo Park. He was willing to pay.

It was functional for everyone. It wasn't elegant. But it worked somehow.

Before long, Mehran called to let him know he'd have to return to Tehran to get a visa for Italy so he could join his friend there. He asked if he could stay with Issa while he waited for it to come through.

"You don't wish to stay at your own place with Ramin?"

It was a pointless question, since Hayat was living there now with Ramin. They had become a couple.

Even as he considered all of this, Issa felt the strangenesses—he found no other word for it—that he had sparked by running into Mehran more than half a year earlier in the language class he taught. Yet he had visited Ramin and Hayat in their apartment and seen in their faces what they were—pure happiness, or perhaps simply a deep gentleness and relief between two otherwise marginalized people.

But then he'd return home after his visits with those two and get shit-faced drunk, thinking: *You lost out in the business of love to a man without a* kir, *and you managed that . . . where? In the Islamic Republic. You deserve a special medal for this.*

On the telephone, he said to Mehran, "Yes, yes. Of course you can stay with me."

"Marco, my Italian, is good to me, you know."

"I don't need explanations, Mehran *jaan*. As long as you're happy."

Mehran told him the two of them had gone to the southern coast of Turkey together. And yes, he was happy so far with the Italian. But no, he still wasn't sure if he could simply leave Tehran for good. It was an admission that took Issa by surprise.

"Why do you think you might not leave Tehran?"

"Tehran is like a bad marriage one gets trapped in."

"This is precisely why you should leave."

"You of all people, Issa. How can you say this? You're the one who came back."

WHEN ISSA AT LAST went to pick up Babacar from the airport, he was still musing on Mehran's words. In the back of the cab on the way home, he asked Babacar again why he would want to come here at all.

"Discipline."

"I don't get why you'd come to the Middle East to find discipline, Baba. But I figure you will tell me."

"I will, my brother. But now I am late for my prayer."

"Yes, we would not want you to be late for your prayer. Do you ever think about anything else but your late prayers?"

"Do not make fun. You remind me of those people who came

to the hotel. Remember the fun they made of my prayer in the lobby at night?"

"Baba, I haven't forgotten. And I am not those people. But I do wish to know one thing: is it the Shia prayer that you now perform or still the Sunni prayer?"

"You make fun again."

"It's a sincere question. Jesus!"

"Yes, your name is Jesus," Baba said with a smile.

On the second day, Issa took him on a road trip, and everywhere they went people would gather around the imposing *siyah*. Baba would humor the curious, sometimes reciting entire chapters of the Koran by heart. Complete strangers in ancient cities like Esfahan, Yazd, and Shiraz invited them into their homes. Baba entertained. Singing in his native Wolof or in French, and even reciting the sonnets of Shakespeare that he had taken up at last. The two put themselves on display, and Baba didn't mind it one bit. Nor did Issa. Babacar was a breath of fresh air, really. A timely miracle from another world who had suddenly parachuted here. The West African's friendship had never allowed for limits. In New York, he had once put himself between what turned out to be a thief's toy gun and the front desk where Issa was busy doing the hotel accounts at three in the morning. "What if the gun had been real?"

"Où sont les neiges d'antan?"

"Are you mad? What do the snows of yesteryear have to do with anything?"

"Life is short. Babacar knows how to take at least one bullet for a friend."

And he'd meant it. In a place as lonely as America, where

neither of them could get much traction on anything, that willingness to take a bullet meant the world. Yes, two men finding each other. Such a rarity.

"Issa, I want to stay in your country for a time."

"Do you still want to become a cleric here? I mean, if you do, it is actually not impossible that we could arrange something. I can't promise, but I'll try. It would mean a lot of studying, though. Years of it. And the snows of yesteryear, my friend, have already melted."

Babacar beamed. He upped his deep voice a notch and sang: "*Each morn a thousand roses brings, you say, but where leaves the rose of yesterday?*"

"You really are crazy."

"All men have the same sorrows. François Villon, Frenchman; Omar Khayyam, Persian. They say the same things at different times in different places. The snow of yesteryear, the rose of yesterday. I am always doing homework, Issa. I am always learning. If I have been unhappy, and sometimes I was, it was because of my size. My unhappiness was the size of me. Do you not remember how people were always gaping at me in the hotel? Of course you do. I was a giant African. A Black giant. So I read Villon and Khayyam and learn languages to make myself *moins terrifiant*. Yes? But I do not always succeed."

"You read because you are a cultured man. Because the words of the world are beauty. And because poetry speaks to you across oceans. You do not read to become less scary, Baba. Come on."

"Yes, all of those things you say are true. But I also read to be less scary. And I do not mind this. I had an idea back in Dakar, but it has now gone silent. It does not give me pain anymore."

"What idea?"

"To go deep. Into the religion. Because it has the words. To study again. I thought to myself: *I will go to the place of my friend Issa. I will go to where Omar Khayyam sang.* Maybe François Villon was Persian in his heart. How do we know? We do not. The souls travel. I imagined another Babacar, not the Babacar that was me in Dakar, or in America. And now I see there was no pain in me. There was only desire. And I was right about something. Here, you make me happy."

"How do I make you happy?"

"You try very hard, even when you are miserable. And you are *souvent*—miserable, my brother. Your trying not to be miserable makes me happy."

"Oh, well, thank you for that."

"Do not feel bad because of what I have said. Men are miserable. Men like us. But we try. It is our—"

"Burden?"

"Yes. That word."

"I could hug you now."

"Yes, you must."

Nothing in life was impossible. Babacar had arrived. It was real.

"You understand you're a novelty here and people love us, love *you*, but it will wear off. They are amazed by your size. In America, they were afraid of you; here you are a show. I apologize."

"My size is a novelty everywhere. And, Issa, fuck you! I am staying here. I need discipline."

"What in god's name does that even mean?"

"I went back to Senegal in shame. Do you understand? Because to them I did not come back rich. I could not live with this. It is boring. Shame is boring."

"And now?"

"I start again. Like I've been planted in the ground for the first time."

They rode across the sprawling Gulf coast from one end of it to the other. There was that infinite ease and wanderlust about Baba. Issa watched him catch up on his prayers in the moonscapes by the sea in the Baluchistan province next to Pakistan and thought that if this moment on earth was possible then anything was. And then he was grateful again, for Baba being here. The West may have kicked them out, but the world was not that small a place after all, and there was still room for them to make things interesting for themselves.

Back at the red beach on Hormuz Island, Baba said, "This place is holy to you. I can tell."

"My older brother brought me here the first time years ago. I was just a teenager."

"Where is this brother?"

"Gone. Dead."

"Why did you never tell me?"

"You were always busy studying your English."

"Don't be stupid, Issa. What did your brother say to you here on this red beach?"

"He said one day they'd build five-star hotels right here and men like you and me would work the night shift for the rich again."

"I think he meant seven-star hotels. I hate hotels."

. . .

BACK IN TEHRAN, the city was still burning. Baba insisted they go to a demonstration. Issa didn't say no, even though he was sure it was a bad idea. How many times had he been at this same exact juncture, thousands screaming their freedom chants and several dozen armed men, at times himself included, facing them with numb eyes? Fear and anger was what the numbness was, and if that young woman who wanted to stick a flower in your helmet or put one on your riot shield had any idea how you felt just then she would get the fuck out of your line of vision with quickness. It was not so different than sparring in a karate tournament, not for a stupid trophy but for real blood. Naïveté rubbed him wrong, especially his own. Freedom might mean that you had nothing left to lose. Except that you could always lose more. There was an infinite well of possibilities for losing more. And it was just as well that the demonstrators he and Babacar ran into at every main boulevard did not realize this, or they'd all shoot themselves in the head even before the riot police did.

At the Karim-Khan Bridge, they were suddenly surrounded by a squad of special police on motorcycles, paired details armed to the teeth, a cross between ice hockey players and evolved giant insects.

"Issa, what should we do now?"

"We need to get the hell out of here. If we fight, they'll break our teeth and they'll deport you. That's if they don't throw you in jail for a few months first."

He could see it in their eyes; the antiriot cops were just more cutting-edge versions of himself when he'd been a recruit and had to keep demonstrators from getting out of hand. He didn't care for them. But he didn't despise them either. He understood what they were and why. The lead detail looked from Issa to Babacar, then gestured with his head—*Get out of here and take this clueless foreign giant with you before things get ugly.* Behind the helmet and the body armor, Issa could still see something of himself in the other guy. The fellow was giving them a chance to get away.

Issa pulled Babacar toward him and they wrestled past the chanting demonstrators toward the street that led to Artists' Park.

"Issa, what do these people want?"

"Freedom."

Babacar began to laugh.

"What is so damn funny?"

"Who is free? Remember when our boss at the hotel would come in late at night worried because there are empty rooms? The man has more money than King Midas and he's still worried about empty rooms. No one is free. It's foolish."

They continued on down the road toward the park. The commotion they'd just encountered—people setting garbage cans and motorcycles on fire—contrasted with the absolute quiet of this street. It was as if the area was holding its breath. The city a sleeping animal. Moments of violence and chaos alongside the eerie stillness that came from fear.

Then it happened. Two regular police cars, not the antiriot uniforms, were idling in the middle of the street. A half dozen cops stood around a tree just inside the park where a young woman had climbed up a few branches and taken her hijab off and set it on fire. She was small, her hair cut short, and she looked like some kind of odd fruit that had materialized on that tree. Just beneath her was a Ping-Pong table. A policeman stood on it, trying to talk the woman down. Several old men a little farther off in the park played badminton. The atmosphere was hardly tense, more like some unlikely tableau vivant.

When Issa had first returned two years ago, there had been a public hanging right there in that very spot where the cop cars were haphazardly parked. He'd come to the hanging out of curiosity. Three guys caught for armed robbery had been raised and strangled from mechanical cranes. An obscene capital punishment. Two minutes before the cranes did their thing, one of the young men made a last request for a glass of water to quench his thirst. The famous George Orwell essay on a similar hanging had come to Issa's mind just then. The condemned man in that other hanging steps around a puddle to avoid getting wet on his way to the noose. The implausibility of it all—the hangings, the puddle of water in Orwell's essay, the request for water here, and now this woman protesting having to wear a hijab in the Islamic Republic climbing up that tree while old men played badminton and what looked like a rookie cop stood on top of a Ping-Pong table telling the woman to "get off Satan's donkey and come down before the antiriot forces make your life and ours miserable."

The cops, it was obvious, wanted none of this. They wanted to go home and be with their families. They didn't get paid enough for this bullshit. The woman shouted something about how she'd do more than burn her hijab—she'd burn herself if she had the nerve—and insisted that she would not come down. Now that her hijab was ashes, she had nothing to stuff on top of her head, and she was perfectly fine with that. The cops laughed. She could have been their sister or daughter. A few passersby tried to stop and give the woman moral support, but the bored cops shooed them off without much force.

Issa stood there mesmerized for a moment. When he finally snapped out of it, he saw that Babacar was walking straight into that confused huddle. He ran after him.

When the cops first laid eyes on Babacar, every single one of them, including the one on the Ping-Pong table, did a double take. He went right up to the foot of the tree and began talking to the woman, who spoke back to him in broken French. Something about the unfairness of the country and how the hijab was an insult to her very being. Issa didn't quite understand it and didn't care one way or another. He wanted Baba and himself out of there. As he grabbed Baba's arm, the policeman on the table reached for a branch and then quickly took hold of one of the woman's legs. Her screams were terrifying. The atmosphere had turned suddenly nasty. This was how these things always played out.

Now a policeman was bear-hugging Issa from behind. No doubt they saw him and Babacar as the cause of the sudden mayhem. A baton came down on his forearm and he had to let go of Babacar. When the cop tried to hit him a second time, Babacar clipped the weapon out of the man's hand and tossed it far into the park. The cop, terrified of what Babacar might do next, took a step back.

The damage, however, had been done.

Nineteen

They stood in the courtyard of the local *kalantari*, not accused of much of anything except that they were busybodies who had caused headache for regular cops dealing with a hijab-burning heroine in a tree.

Yet even at the police station, Babacar turned the whole thing into his usual one-man show. He did his Koran recitation spiel, and after a while every cop there wanted a selfie or a video with him. When Jafar finally showed up to get them out of there, a sort of sadness came over the place. The cops had fallen for Babacar. How did the man manage to draw these feelings out of people?

"What happened to your arm?" Jafar asked. "Why are you holding it like that?"

Issa turned to his friend, who looked less frail than he had in years, coaxed at last out of a bubble of addiction and physical pain.

"I took a baton for the women of our lovely and very just country. The arm's not broken. Just hurts a bit."

"And this big guy?"

"He's my former colleague."

An hour later, Jafar took them all back to Aziz's house, where Solmaz, Ramin, and Hayat had all gathered and were waiting. They were relieved to see that Issa hadn't suffered a worse fate, and at once delighted and mystified by the West African's presence. When Baba announced that his prayers were late, Aziz fetched a prayer rug and seal.

"Nana, he doesn't need the seal."

"No?"

"He's not a Shia. Not yet anyway."

"Then why is he here?"

"People come here for all kinds of reasons, Nana. Anyway, he's got it in his head he wants to become Shia. So maybe you should give him the seal after all."

"Become Shia to achieve what, really?" Hayat now asked.

"Better theater perhaps? Or maybe he thinks the family of the Prophet got a raw deal."

"Who doesn't get a raw deal?" Jafar pitched in, and both Solmaz and Ramin nodded.

"Look, all this man needs is to know where the *qibla* is so he can pray in the right direction to Mecca. That's all. As long as I've known the guy, he's always concerned about saying his prayers late."

"A man who prays is never late," Jafar observed.

"Amen," Hayat added.

As Babacar went to the corner of the yard to do his ablutions and then faced *qibla* to pray, Aziz made tea and the two pairs of lovers—Solmaz and Jafar, and Hayat and Ramin—held each other's hands, as if an expedition were finally complete, a journey ended, and they all had somehow, despite insurmountable odds, survived.

. . .

AZIZ WOULD NOT TAKE no for an answer. She wanted a real ceremony for her daughter, Madam Doctor Solmaz—a white-dress wedding with lots of photographs. They had to humor their matriarch. That meant ten days later the very same group arrived at a cleric's marriage office in the Poonak district, on the other side of town, where the red-bearded turban had said he could arrange for a dozen extras to show up at a make-believe ceremony between Solmaz and Jafar in his garden behind the office. It was going to cost Jafar a fortune to pay for perfect strangers to come up to Issa to congratulate him on the marriage of his "sister." But Issa had a better idea. He made a single phone call, and on the day of the wedding a cast right out of one of Hashem's plays showed up.

Masti, looking regal as ever in a pink straw sun hat, said, "You did right to call me, Issa. You can see that Her Loveliness still has some bones in her. Thank you very much."

"You are more than lovely, dear Masti. Thank you for bringing these people today."

"I would not have missed it for the world. Is it a real marriage?"

"It's not unreal. It's just overdue and we were in a hurry."

"And Mehran? Where is he?"

"He may have found love elsewhere."

"You'll make me cry, Issa. Truly?"

"I pray for it."

Masti spread her arms as if to embrace the universe. "I want a thousand pictures from today, Issa. Today is the first day of every day."

As always, Babacar turned into the life of the party. Masti and her gang of actors were smitten with him. At some point, Issa looked down from the balcony and listened as Baba and Masti recited the poetry of Omar Khayyam in Persian and English:

> Ah, my beloved, fill the cup that clears
> today of past regrets and future fears.
> Tomorrow? Why, tomorrow I may be
> myself with yesterday's seven thousand years.

> There was the door to which I found no key;
> there was the veil through which I might not see.
> Some little talk awhile of me and thee
> there was—and then no more of thee and me.

And then there was the red-bearded cleric, wide-eyed but admirably game in his own limited way, given the circumstances of this invented wedding that he had just officiated. The holy man's world had suddenly leaped into the unknown. Who were these people, and who was that giant man from another world and that manwoman wearing an enormous pink hat while reciting Khayyam? The cleric rubbing his face as if he might soon wake from a dream, and Issa watching him and listening to poetry a thousand years old and thinking that this setup surely had to be the strangest of all the strange things that had happened this past year.

But things did get stranger. While Issa was tied up trying to figure out the paperwork to convert the dojo into a language school, Babacar ended up spending more time with Hayat and Ramin. They had an easy rapport and their conversations would often devolve into howling laughter.

There was a cheerfulness to it that made Issa hungry for it again, love—love in all its twists and turns, its pining, its messiness, and, conversely, its consistency. Sometimes Babacar and Hayat would spend long stretches of time taking turns reciting the Holy Book from memory. Competing. Babacar's deep tenor vying with Hayat's exquisite Arabic. Ramin, in a corner of their living room, read online about various car engines while the other two went on and on with their Koranic recitations. It was odd, dreamlike, bizarre, and somehow right. It was the Islamic Republic in all its unlikeliness and lies and contradictions and occasional transcendence.

At the make-believe marriage ceremony, he'd asked Solmaz how it was going to work out now with her son.

"I'm going to be seeing him more than ever before. You know, Issa, there's nothing more fulfilling than being with someone who is capable."

"Yes, Jafar is quite capable. He was just lacking a motive all these years. Now he has one."

"Thank you, Issa. Thank you for bringing us together."

"It was an accident. You both showed up at my door while I wasn't there, remember?"

"Even so. And look at how happy my mother is for a change. Thank you for this wedding. Thank you for all the people you asked to come."

"Will Nana want to see her grandson now?"

"She'll give it time. Not right away. She does not trust men."

"An understatement."

Then one afternoon, when he went to pick up Babacar from Ramin and Hayat's apartment, he saw a look on the couple's faces that told him something was afoot.

"What?"

Babacar said in English, "I stay here, Issa. With these two."

"You know their story, right?" Issa muttered back in English.

"I know. They have told me. And they have told me also the Imam gave a fatwa. It is all good. *Alhamdulillah.*"

Hayat brought a bottle of *arak* and set it in front of Issa with a shot glass.

"You'll need this, Mr. Issa."

Ramin put a hand on his shoulder. "We need Baba. And Baba needs us."

"I'm already willing to listen to you three. Don't make it so damn theatrical."

Babacar came and sat opposite him. Hayat and Ramin stayed back, hovering by the window.

Baba said, "Why do you drink that devil stuff? You are a Muslim."

"It allows me to feel guilt. And then I become a better Muslim for a while. Anyway, let's get on with it."

"I will stay here."

"That has already been established. But why? Don't get me wrong, I am very happy you are here with us. But I still cannot divine why you really came here, to Tehran."

"I had no place else to go."

"Dakar seems to me like a perfectly good place to be. I wouldn't mind being there myself."

"Yes, but you are not from there. I am."

"Are we back to the subject of shame again?"

"Yes. Shame. When they threw me out of America, I went back to Dakar. Then what? I am this failure to my family. Before, I am sending them money. I support everybody. Big family. Now they think I failed. That I'm no good. Not easy for me to live there."

"What do you care what people think, Baba?"

"I care. We care about everything. When somebody says they don't care, you know they care. You took me to the red beach on Persian Gulf—why? Because you care. Memory cares. Today cares. Tomorrow cares. We are people who care. Suffering is not what we wish. We are not Buddha."

The man had made his point.

"So you just abandoned the big family back in Senegal?"

"The big family, they needed a lesson. Next time I go back there, they will appreciate me again."

"And what do you think is waiting for you here?"

Babacar smiled. "Marriage."

"Come again?"

Babacar motioned Ramin and Hayat to the table as he got up to trade places with them.

Issa took two generous shots of the *arak*. It steeled him. He knew what was coming and it was fine. Everything was fine. He wondered when Mehran would be arriving from Beirut or Turkey or wherever he was with his Italian lover this minute. It had a ring, *Italian lover.* He could use an Italian lover himself. He should have stayed in Beirut and found himself someone. Instead all he'd found there were the Hezbollah guys wanting to kick his ass or maybe recruit him or both. He wondered what Nasser was doing right now? Cruising in front of Daneshjoo Park? Being mean to his new wife? Issa took another swig of the *arak* and his head began a lazy swim. Those Afghan boys in Zamzam dancing for the older guys.

It had made him sick to see it. But who was he to judge? He'd wanted to burn a building down and in his place the Afghan foreman had done the job. Made life and conscience easy for him. He should go to Zamzam again and see what the man whose wife burned herself was up to. *Maybe I'll burn his place down again and again.* Every time the son of a whore rebuilt the place, Issa would burn it down. Or better yet, he'd have the Rilke-quoting Afghan foreman burn it down.

Ramin said, "Agha Issa, you feel all right?"

"Of course not."

"All we want to do is make things work for everybody."

"I'm not your judge. And I'm listening, am I not?"

"Hayat needs a husband. I can't marry her legally until you know what. But I've decided I don't want to go through with the procedure."

"Getting a *kir* between your legs, you mean?"

"Yes, that. I don't need it."

"You can have mine. It's useless for me anyway."

"Please. Take this seriously."

Issa nodded. He downed another shot.

"Hayat needs a husband because one never knows. One of her brothers might eventually come for her."

"I know. You can't marry her because you are without a *kir*, and the law won't allow you to marry with that minor absence."

"But Babacar could marry Hayat. If he marries Hayat, then we can get him a residency here in this country. He can stay. And then everyone is happy."

Issa laughed without a trace of mirth. "You think all that will be easy here?"

Hayat spoke. "It is not easy. We know. We were hoping you could speak to Agha Jafar about it. He could help."

"I see. You need my help to smooth the way for this marriage."

"Would you do it?"

"*Lanat bar shaitan*, and a curse on the devil! Since all of you have gone utterly mad, why not? I'll see what I can do."

ISSA CAME OUT of their apartment alone again. Baba-less, and slightly drunk. It was early evening now. A brisk second half of December. Bahar Street was busy. The Armenian sausage joint had a line out the door. You could feel Christmas in the air of this old Christian neighborhood. He walked the length of Bahar all the way to where the high-end children's clothing boutiques began. The area was flooded in light, and families were strolling in and out of the shops. Not many were buying, though. Not many had the money to buy. It was as if the city was going through the motions of normalcy. But there was so much destitution. When he'd left for the United States, it was rare to see many beggars on the streets. More than a decade later, this metropolis had tumbled into a storm of unrelenting poverty.

He continued on down south toward the Grand Bazaar, and before long he was back on Aziz's street. A lone lamp shone a sick light on the alley where the ubiquitous junkies huddled around one of their own. The old guy that they fussed over looked ghostly.

"Overdose?" Issa asked.

"No, Agha Issa *jaan*," one of the thin young junkies said. He pointed to Aziz's door. "Our *khanum* told him he could not stay here on this street anymore. And he went and took a few pills. We don't know what pills this time. But he'll come around. This old man is made of bricks. Nothing kills him."

"Does Aziz *khanum* know the state he's in?"

"No, sir. And we will not tell her. She's our mother. This man is a fool. We'll fix him. Tomorrow when Aziz *khanum* brings us tea, she'll forgive him. This happens maybe twice a year."

Issa stood there in disbelief. "Twice a year?"

"Yes, Agha Issa *jaan*," another one of the men said. "This man's a Turk. Like her. What can we tell you? Happens at least once every other season. It's like a contract between the two of them."

One of the men asked for a *salawat*, and together they all chorused the salutation to the Prophet.

He decided not to knock on the door and turned around.

Daneshjoo Park was busy as always. A show at the big theater had just ended, and scores of people were streaming outside. Issa sat on a bench and waited. Maybe Nasser would show up. A quickie at the end of his shift before going back to his wife. A year ago, he had thought of Nasser as a brother. Now he had little feeling toward the man one way or another.

Your nonexistence is as loyal to me as your existence. Issa thought about the words Hayat had once translated from an old Arabic text in one of those journals. While the meaning was still inscrutable, he thought he was as close to them now as he'd ever be.

It was getting to be late in the evening. He continued his walk, passing couples who were still playing badminton at Artists' Park. Here the theater let out even later. *Antigone.* Just beyond, men played volleyball near where that young woman had climbed a tree and burned her hijab in protest. Did anyone even remember that two years earlier, men had been hung from those fucking cranes right there? Three young men lifted into the air simultaneously and dead within a fraction of a second. None of that bullshit of kicking your feet in the air while struggling not to die, like in the movies. The mercilessness was so thorough that the nineteen-year-old conscripts tasked with keeping the crowds back could not even turn to face the cranes and the dead. Such a symphony of unfairness that the crowd fell silent at first. Then, after a few seconds, the ear-piercing wails of the mothers and sisters of the condemned. The crowd imagining that that picture of death could be any of them. Issa wondered where that young hijab-burner was now—at home? In a jail cell? Quickly married off by her family so that she would settle down and stop being such a nuisance to everybody?

His cell phone buzzed. A text message from Nasser. The man seemed always to be hovering and on Issa's trail—at the airport when Issa came back from Beirut, at the theater that night with Masti, and now just as he'd entered Issa's thoughts after so long. *Let's not be strangers. I want you to visit us. My wife is pregnant. I want us to celebrate. You are my brother.*

But what about Daneshjoo Park?

Nasser didn't answer for a few minutes. Then: *I am not committing a crime. Not hurting anyone. It's a life inside my life.*

Maybe Nasser was going about this the right way after all. All Issa had ever known with his old man and his brother was men struggling with their own shadows and desires. Nasser wasn't a beast; he was just another anxious guy afraid of being found out and losing his captainship at some godforsaken firehouse in the godforsaken Zamzam district.

I'll come to visit your family whenever you want, Issa wrote. *And, congrats. Mubarak.*

IN THE MORNING, a bit hungover and still sleepy, he opened the door to Mehran's knock.

"Why didn't you tell me you were on your way? I would have picked you up at the airport."

Exhausted from his journey, Mehran excused himself to freshen up. After emerging from a long shower with a towel wrapped around his waist and another around his head, he finally came and lay down next to Issa. He picked up a thin book that was open face-down on the bed and read out loud: *"If you listen to the 'times,' they will tell you in a low voice not to speak in their name, but to be silent in their name."*

"Yes," Issa murmured, staring at the ceiling. "Silence."

"We are awkward, you and me. You know? Are you still sorry you slept with me in Beirut?"

"It was actually in Mount Lebanon. And no, I was never sorry."

Mehran turned the book over and read its title out loud: *The Writing of the Disaster.* "Can I ask you something, Issa?"

"Sure."

"Why do you read such grim books?"

"It's not mine. Almost everything here was my brother's. Including this." He pointed at the book.

"But it's lying on your bed now. You're the one reading the book, not Hashem who's been dead so long."

"What is your point, *azizam*?"

Mehran tossed the book aside and put a hand to his mouth in mock exaggeration. "You are calling me darling?"

"So I did."

Mehran took the towel off his head and squeezed his face into Issa's chest.

"And what are we doing now?" Issa asked.

"We could kiss."

"What about your Italian?"

"Issa."

"What?"

"I'm not going back to Italy. Or to Beirut or Turkey or anywhere else. I'm staying right here."

"You mean at my house?"

"If you'll have me."

"And why would you want to do that? I mean, why would you pass up the opportunity to go somewhere better?"

"There are no better places, Issa *jaan*. Stay anywhere long enough, be with anyone long enough, and all the warts start to show. I may as well stay in my own country for that. I'm not made for elsewhere. I found that out on this trip. I'm glad I went and stayed away for a while. But I'm not leaving again. I need my rituals."

"You can have your rituals in Rome or Naples or wherever that guy was from."

"I didn't like his lips."

"What?"

"His lips. I didn't like them."

"Are you serious?"

"Lips are important. Come, I'll show you."

Mehran smelled like lavender. Random thoughts went through

Issa's head. At one time, he'd imagined he wanted to be a commando and serve with Jafar and Ahmad Shah Massoud in Afghanistan. Before that, he'd taken for granted that he'd follow in his father's footsteps and run the karate academy. In America, he had done the graveyard shift with Babacar and thought about getting a PhD in comparative literature, maybe a minor in critical theory so he could bullshit his way to a respectable academic job in some nowhere town. Then there was the habit he'd picked up: The drugs. The methadone. Cops holding him for a bunch of Xanax pills that everybody and their mother took nowadays. The world was fucked up, unjust. All the burned women of the world. All the burned men in all the wars happening around them. The burned house in Zamzam. The Afghan foreman. Rilke and his burned poems. Writings of the disaster, all of it. His brother dead and this big, empty apartment, too much for him alone by himself.

And here he was being kissed by Mehran lightly on the lips and taking in that hungry lavender scent. He could have cried.

Mehran said, "You don't really want to kiss me, do you? You're doing it out of sympathy."

"What's wrong with sympathy? People do things for all kinds of reasons."

"Am I a charity case, then, Issa?"

"You already know the answer to that. You are absolutely not a charity case."

"Then kiss me for real."

"Later."

Mehran sighed and pressed his face back into Issa's chest and stayed there. "Do you think we could get along?"

"Haven't we so far?"

"Yes, but this is different."

"I suppose if Ramin and Hayat and my African friend whom you haven't yet met can get along, so can you and I."

"Issa."

"I'm listening."

"Do you feel your brother's ghost here sometimes?"

"Not just his. My old man's too."

Mehran remained there, pressed into Issa's chest like it was a pillow.

"Nasser wouldn't let me live in Zamzam. You think you could really have me in Monirieh?"

"Yes, I can have you in Monirieh, Mehran *jaan*."

"As what?"

"As my disaster."

"Be serious."

"You can stay as long as you wish."

"Because you want me?"

"Because you are here."

"And that's a good enough reason?"

"Most of human history is nothing but that, people just happening to be where they are."

They stayed silent. This building was exhausted. This neighborhood. Everything.

"Issa, let me make you a promise."

"What do you promise?"

"I won't take a lot of space here in this ghost home of yours."

"Please do. Take the space. Fill it, if you can."

ACKNOWLEDGMENTS

This book of fiction owes its life and thanks to a number of people: to Habibe, for gifting the vastness of the Persianate universe; to Maryam in Tehran, for lifting a veil on the breathtaking classics of the Arab world; to Rana, for offering an elegant key to Africa; to my everlasting anchors in New York, Maryam and Ashil; to Alimorad, who embodies a life in literature; and to Kira, who holds the earth together.

I also wish to thank the City College of New York for having made this writing life possible for so long. And I am deeply grateful to the entire team at Viking Penguin. Lastly, and most importantly, a special acknowledgment to the two people who have trusted and worked with me every step of the way over the years: my very dear and longtime agent, Jessica Papin, and a one-of-a-kind editor and enduring friend, Ibrahim Ahmad.